Erotic Short Stories For Women Written by Men

Explicit Adult Erotica Featuring First Times, Threesomes, MILFs, Daddy, Anal Sex, Pegging, Gang Bangs, Cuckold, Older-Younger, BDSM, and more...

Rayna Russell

indirect, which are incurred as a result of the use of the information contained within this document, including, but not limited to, — errors, omissions, or inaccuracies.

Contents

Introduction

Hello friends,

It's your old pal Rayna, editor for this collection of sexy stories and several other collections as well.

You know me, I always ask for feedback; it helps me figure out what kind of material really gets you going. Well, interestingly, I had several of you tell me that the stories that turned you on the most in my previous collections... were the stories written and narrated by men. One reader told me that these stories allowed her to listen in to the thoughts of a man, and she found that very erotic.

So I said to myself: why not reach out to several of my favorite male writers (and narrators for the audiobook) and give the people what they want!?

And, wow, did they deliver!

In this collection, you'll get a *wide* range of stories:

You'll get a sweet and sexy first-time story and a story about rediscovering sex after a bad breakup. You'll meet a young man obsessed with the MILF he met at the store and a young woman and her smoking hot sugar daddy.

My writers do not hold back! There are also some really raunchy tales - gang bangs, cuckolding, anal sex, and even pegging.

I promise: this book will leave you breathless. And it will give you a real glimpse into the brains of horny men.

And if you still want more, don't forget to check out my other books. Just search for "Rayna Russell" on Amazon and Audible.

And, as always, you can reach out at any time with your feedback or if you want to submit a story for consideration in my next collection. (Three thousand words is the sweet spot.)

Sit back, relax, and enjoy!

XOXO,

Rayna

RaynaRussellErotica@gmail.com

Chad and the Milf
By Leo Marcus

An apple a day keeps the pain away. The mental pain, at least. It was a sentence that I told myself often because I had everything I wanted, and yet I still felt empty. I was empty, unlike the place that I was in.

The supermarket. I always felt most human in the supermarket. Like I didn't need to be on. I could just be Chad, hanging out in produce without needing to look sexy, corporate, whatever the case may be. I could just be a guy looking at grapes. It may sound weird to say that at times I felt like I needed to feel sexy. But that pertained to picking up women. I always just wanted to look my best.

I hadn't gotten to the grapes yet, though. I was still by the apples. Fittingly, I was still picking apples out. I took my time in the produce section because it was the one thing that I could control. Unlike many people, and this wasn't a put-down, I felt like I was in control of my health. It was the one area of my life that I could predict. Sure, things could always go south, and I could be diagnosed with some terrible illness. Well, until then, I'd liked to believe that I was in control of my destiny. I had to believe that because I owned a gym. If I wasn't healthy and if I didn't believe in myself like that, how could I ever expect anyone to come in and shell out twenty dollars a month to work out in my business? I couldn't. And I wouldn't.

This was why I had a thriving business. Because of my mentality outside of the business. I took care of myself. I rarely partied. I had as much sex with as many women as I wanted. There wasn't much to complain about. For a 25-year-old man, I was pretty damn accomplished. And I knew that without being egocentric. I knew my worth, and I knew what I could bring to the table for people. At the end of the day, there was just this element that was missing. I couldn't put my finger on what it was, but on the regular, even while in the produce section chillin' I felt like I was missing something. As it turned out, you could have everything in the world and still feel empty. I guess that was the ongoing irony of life.

In any case, I picked out a few apples and put them in my cart. I let out a deep breath, kicked myself for dwelling on negatives, and moved on to the grapes.

Green or red. There was a micro decision that felt like a chore. I wasn't sure what it was, but I suddenly felt drained. I guess the whole thinking about stuff deeply while in the grocery store wasn't doing me any favors.

I needed to stop. I needed to regulate my thoughts. It wasn't rare that I got down on myself from time to time. Just like when you have everything in life, and there's that emptiness, the same thing happens when you have these cycles of happiness versus sadness. I went through them like everyone else. As much as I tried to be a perfect human, I couldn't be. The whole having a void thing just had a way of creeping up on me at times. And I still didn't have a mechanism for dealing with it. It was too difficult. I would throw myself into either sport, looking at stocks and flirting with women. Whatever I could do to distract myself from what I was feeling, I would do it tenfold.

At that moment, I took a few grapes and plucked

them into my mouth. I was going with red. I had eaten the red one and the green one. The red one tickled my taste buds a little bit more.

"You're supposed to pay for those before you eat them. Because now who's going to want that batch of green after your mitts have been all over them?"

I turned to my right and noticed a beautiful black woman whose only flaw was looking at me with anger. It wasn't often that someone far shorter than me had something to say with such vigor. My muscles tended to keep me in my own type of safe space. Now when it came to this woman, I wasn't going to go off on her. Because at the end of the day, she was a woman. And I wasn't going to ignore her because she was stunning. She had these thick, luscious lips. Her eyes were wide despite the anger. She was wearing a white T-shirt that showed the color of her bra underneath. But that wasn't what I noticed most; it was the size of her breasts. They somehow looked like they had implants and were natural at the same time.

It all came down to what type of comeback I wanted to give her. Did I want it to be witty? Did I want to be sarcastic? Or did I just want it to be manly and guttural? The fact that I was running through all these different options in my head meant that I was unhealthily invested. I guess I kind of cared what she thought of me. "So what are you, the grape police? This must be the department of the police that is actually attractive."

I flashed her a devious smirk to let her know that I wasn't being confrontational.

"If you think I'm going to give you the time of day after you just stole a bunch of grapes, then you're absolutely nothing more than a meathead with no brain."

Well. I'd be lying if I said that I wasn't caught off guard a little bit. I had made a vow with myself not to be confrontational, but she was super confrontational. She had such spice to her words. There was such a fire in her tone. "Ouch. Getting really uptight about a couple of grapes. What's really going on with your day?"

She shook her head and looked away from me. There was something sexy even about that little movement. I guess I liked the thrill of the chase. I also liked really strong women, and I wasn't just talking about the ones who went to the gym. She had this demeanor about her that told me she was running her life. You know when you meet someone and they're just not in control of anything? I was a big proponent of being in control. That's why I liked working out. You made your muscles bigger. You took control of your health. And she carried herself like that without even really having to do anything. I was interested. Heck, I was more than interested. I wanted to fuck her.

"Let's not kid ourselves and pretend that you care about my day. All I'm saying is maybe you shouldn't gnaw on things that other people are going to buy."

I held up the red grapes. And then I grabbed the green grapes before putting them in my cart. "Look at that. I'm going to buy them both. Does that make you feel better? See I'm considerate. I just need my flaws pointed out to me. Maybe that could be your job. I would just need your number for that."

Given her sexy complexion, I couldn't necessarily see if her cheeks were going red. But the smirk on her face was enough to tell me that I had penetrated those thick walls of hers. I liked pulling away those layers even after just knowing her for three seconds. It made me feel a little accomplished that I could do that.

"You're not used to people saying no to you, huh? Do muscles trick people into thinking you're filled with a nice personality?"

I didn't allow any of the muscles in my face to move at that comment. She was trying to rattle me.

That was fine. Someone like her, I wasn't expecting an easy dialogue. And anyway, I enjoyed the challenging banter.

"What you see is what you get. At least I'm being authentic. You're the one who seems a little guarded. Defensive over grapes, actually. But you're kind of like me as well. Because you shoot from the hip. Someone that shoots from the hip would say something like, 'I think you're the most beautiful woman in the supermarket' right now."

She gave me a look as if she didn't want to look at me. But she had no control over it. And that's how I knew I had won her over.

Don't ask me how, but I was in her bed, and we were making out. Her name was Lucy, and okay I'll tell you how. We continued our chat in the supermarket, and somehow it led to me saying, "I bet I could beat you to your house." And if I won, she had to invite me in. She invited me in, and one thing led to the next. We just had this undeniable chemistry, this spark that could cause a forest fire. And that's why we were making out in her bed. Our clothes were still on, but I had a really strong feeling that they weren't going to be on for a very long time.

"I'm divorced," she said as we were kissing.

I didn't want to stop what we were doing, but what she just said kind of warranted a response, no?

"Why do you feel like you need to tell me this right now? Let me guess: You haven't done this in a very long time."

She pulled off from the kiss and gave me her eyes. "Bingo. I haven't had sex since my divorce. I'm a 45-year-old divorcee, and I don't do this a lot, okay?"

I smiled. "Was that why you were so defensive in the grocery store about grapes?"

I knew she wanted to laugh. I could tell. She was holding it back. And I guess she couldn't hold it back any longer because she kissed me to stop the impulse. I didn't care about her answer. I just cared about putting my tongue in her mouth.

We kissed for a good minute until she pulled off again and said, "I've never gotten with a white man before either." Without me giving her any response, she started to kiss me once more. With all that information swimming in my head, to say that I was a little thrown off was an understatement. But I was a professional and had sex. I didn't mean that in a cocky way; I had just been around. I prided myself on knowing what to do in the bedroom. The next thing that I wanted to do was see her titties.

I lifted her up a little bit and pulled off that T-shirt of hers. There before me were two beautiful big breasts. The anticipation to see them was unlike anything I had experienced in a long time. But that was good. I felt alive compared to the grocery store.

I wasted no time in taking that bra off. And then out flopped those giant breasts of hers. They did a bit of a bounce when they fell. There before me were two very dark nipples. Little that she knew, I had never been with a black woman either. None of that was relevant, but seeing titties like hers in person was new for me. I put one in my mouth and sucked it hard.

She let out a little moan as I sucked. I had one hand on her back and pulled her in closer. Her warmth was euphoric. There was this exhilarating feeling that traveled through my body. I wanted her so badly, yet I was taking her. I moved my hand from her back and squeezed her titty. There was that little moan again.

I couldn't wait much longer. I needed more. So I laid her down and grabbed hold of her jeans. The button specifically. I popped it open with excitement that I tried to contain. Down the zipper and down came the pants. With those pants were the underwear.

When I looked down, I saw nothing but a beautiful pussy. When I opened the lips up, it was glistening pink. My body went into autopilot as I started to lick. Her salty flavor riled me up. While I licked her, I put two fingers inside and pulled them in and out. Her voice went so high-pitched in terms of the moans that she was filling the room with. I could feel the ridges inside of her. The roof of her vagina, I would never forget. I would also never forget how tight she was getting. She was forty-five and divorced, yet her pussy made it seem like she was a virgin.

The more that I licked, the more she pushed her torso toward my face. I welcomed it. I welcomed seeing that hard exterior of hers soften. In a way, I couldn't believe what was happening. One minute we were in the grocery store standing before grapes, the next I was between her legs sticking my tongue in places that I had only been imagining.

"I want to see your dick," she said out of nowhere.

That made my dick go way harder. I mean, it was already hard, but it went way harder after that.

I smiled and rose up a little bit. I took my shirt off first and watched her eyes dance over my body. I waited a few seconds to reveal my dick. Giving her what she wanted, I unbuttoned my pants and unzipped them. With my boxers, I yanked them down and out sprang my seven-inch cock.

She smiled. Without any hesitation, she got up to start stroking me. The next thing I knew, my dick was in her mouth. I was the first white dick she had ever sucked. I took a little pride in that. It was a stupid thing to take pride in. Well, I don't know, I guess I felt like there was some sort of meaning behind it. I guess I felt flattered by it even though I knew I shouldn't have been. The race didn't matter.

When she was finished sucking my cock, I put it in her. In and out I went, hard and fast.

"Faster," she said.

I obliged. It was getting harder to not come. I did my best, but it was getting really difficult every time I looked into her eyes. Luckily for me, her nails dug into my back and her body stiffened. She was coming before me.

With her finished, I gave myself permission to finish too. I pulled out really quickly and came all over her stomach. She smiled again.

While I lay next to her after she'd cleaned herself up, she draped her naked body over me. "I'm not going to lie, that was incredible. But that doesn't stop the fact that I'd be embarrassed to be seen with you. You're too much of a musclehead."

"I thought you'd be embarrassed because I'm a white boy."

She laughed. "No. You're a cool white boy. You just gotta tone down the ego. And then maybe this can work out."

"Oh, baby, I know it's going to work out. I don't know what your ex-husband will do, but I'm going to treat you so much better."

The way that she held me after that I kind of felt like she believed it.

The first time that we went out together officially was to a Louisiana cuisine restaurant. She was from Louisiana and wanted me to see what type of food she grew up with.

"It's got a little bit of a kick, but I like it," I said after taking a bite of my shrimp.

"Look at you, this big musclehead, and you can't take a little spice," she teased.

"Oh baby, I can take a lot of spice. Just look at how I take it personally. That's the spiciest thing of all, no?"

There was that beautiful smile of hers all over again.

"You know, making you smile makes me feel

really accomplished. I don't know why. But let me ask you, are you still embarrassed to be with me out in public?"

She shook her head no while spooning her pasta into her mouth. "You've changed my perception of muscleheads. You make them look cool. And you're very good in bed."

My cheeks went super red when she said that. I wasn't a man who got embarrassed easily. But man, she caught me off guard. "Damn, you really know how to come out of the left field with things. Now I'm the embarrassed one. Am I anything like your ex-husband?"

"You're nothing like my ex-husband. We only had a six-month marriage. I should have known better before marrying him given the fact that we had dated for ten years. It was a tumultuous ten years. We had the type of relationship where one day we were together and then the next we were broken up. Sometimes he would just say really mean things to me, too, and I shouldn't have put up with half of the things he said. You're a sweetheart. I was obviously defensive in the supermarket when I saw a guy like you. But you changed that entire perception for me."

"I'm glad I was able to do that for you, Lucy."

After our date, we went to my place, and we did the same thing that we did at her place. Except it was a lot more rambunctious.

"Oh my God, Chad, yes."

We were doing it doggy style. I had both my hands on her cheeks, and I was squeezing them as I penetrated her. I was really thrusting hard. I had a feeling that we were going to be okay. Something told me that she and I were going to last. Only time would tell, especially given the fact that I was 25 and she was almost double my age. But so far, based on what we had done together, it seemed like we were going to have a happily ever after.

My goal was to one day have sex with her in my gym.

Carly's Gang
By Jim K. Keller

My wife, Carly, was acting strange. I'm not talking about the type of strange where there might be a surprise birthday party being planned. I'm talking about something strange, and I felt on edge about it.

When it comes to home life, there's baseline normalcy that you always want in place. You don't want there to be any tension. You don't want to sense that something is wrong and you need to talk about it with your wife. When it came to Carly, I knew when something was on her mind.

She always defined herself as a strong black woman. The crazy part about that was, she didn't need to do that for the world to know. Because it was the way that she carried herself. It was the way she handled herself in every situation. Unlike me, a brute who had a short temper at times, she carried herself with poise. She would be the definition of dignity. With that being said, being her biggest fan, despite her stoicism at times, I could still tell when something was on her mind. She had like this absent stare. She could be talking to you but look like she was elsewhere. Her eye contact was minimal. And all of these signs were happening right before my eyes.

Over the years, I'd also learned that in times like this, it wasn't best to dive in headfirst. If I wanted to get a straight answer out of her, I needed to come off as not confrontational. As a man, you need to be able to come into a conversation with open ears, and what's more important is conveying that you have open ears. If you come in defensively, you're only going to get defensive back. But of course, knowing that something was bothering my wife, I did feel a little defensive. To remedy that, I just had to figure out what was going on.

We had dinner. It was quieter than usual. Carly ate her meatloaf while staring at the plate. She mushed around her mashed potatoes into the red sauce. This was when I said, "Carly, baby, I know something's wrong. Why don't you just tell me?"

"Nothing's wrong." She blurted it out almost as if

she had been expecting me to say something like that. She was locked and loaded.

"Baby, I've been with you for how many years? What's on your mind? I don't know why you always think that I'm going to lash out or something."

She shrugged. The bites of her food became smaller and faster.

There was no doubt in my mind there was something wrong. And I already knew that it was going to be an uphill battle trying to get the information out of her. I knew my wife. When she didn't want to tell me something, it was very difficult to get it out. It was like cracking open a safe for some sort of high-tech vault. That made me frustrated.

"Baby, I'm not going to pull teeth here. I love you. Just tell me what's going on with you. You're going to drive me crazy."

It would stand that she looked up from her plate and gave me a pair of long eyes. There was frustration in them as she said, "I don't know. I just have these fantasies that I know are wrong, and I need to let them go."

Whoa. It was definitely not what I expected. My heart started to race at the prospect of what she was saying. Because if you really dissected it, you could tell that whatever the fantasy was had nothing to do with me. I would have encouraged any fantasy that she had with me. This one was a problem. She must have been frustrated because it had nothing to do with her husband. So damn, I was worried.

There could only be one. I remembered it from when we had first gotten married. If she still had that fantasy after all these years, then that was going to be something that needed to be taken care of.

"Fantasies. Let me guess, it's the whole getting gangbanged thing?" I asked her.

Her face softened for only a second. And then it reverted back to her restrained frustration. I guess she didn't want to be frustrated about it. That meant that she had shame toward it. Funnily enough, I wasn't as uncomfortable with the idea as she might have thought. "Yeah, but that's not your problem. I know what's wrong. I shouldn't have these fantasies. They've just been, I don't know, on my mind as of late."

What does a man do in a situation like that? Should I encourage her? Was I supposed to be supportive? Was I supposed to put my foot down and throw the marriage card out there so that these types of things didn't happen? Or was marriage supposed to be this thing that we defined and decided for ourselves what was normal? "Baby. I know that you love me at the end of the day. I know that your heart belongs to me. So I don't know, I guess in this case I see it as something you've always wanted to do, and you didn't get to do it before me, and it's something that you want to experience. So I can be supportive of it."

Her face softened even more. There might have even been a little bit of shock mixed in there. I couldn't blame her. "You would really support that?"

"I love you with all my heart. And I know where our relationship stands. So yeah, that's not a part of me that's insecure. I feel like it's a way we can both grow. I know it sounds weird, and I know it's very unexpected, but that's the way I see it."

She smiled and straightened up in her chair. "You really warm my heart." Leaving her chair, she came over to me and gave me a long kiss. I'd be lying if I said that it felt weird to think about those lips kissing someone else. But at the same time, I guess the thought excited me. I guess I wanted to test myself and my own level of confidence.

"So who would we pick to gangbang you?"

She sat back down and gave me this look as though she couldn't believe we were talking about what we were talking about. And I guess I felt the same way. But it wasn't in a bad way. There was a rising excitement in me, but I couldn't quite put my finger on what it was as I had never experienced such a thing. It was an unprecedented situation that I never thought I would be in. It was a situation that I didn't think anyone was prepared for.

"I don't know," she said in a coy way.

I could have been crazy, but I couldn't tell whether or not she already had people in her mind. Once again, my heart started to race. It was crazy to think how a conversation could spark such a feeling. It was such a rollercoaster of emotions. You marry someone and live with them for years, and then suddenly you're in this conversation that gives you goosebumps. Mine were marching up and down like they were a small army. "I feel like you already have people in mind."

She looked down at her plate and shuffled some food around it. That kind of confirmed it for me. "I don't know."

My breath was short when I said to her, "Okay so that look means that you do. Who do you have in mind, baby? Just spill it, all right? We've already gotten this far in the conversation. Don't be afraid of telling me things."

She hesitated before saying, "You promise you're not going to be mad?"

"Well, when you put it that way, my mind is obviously going to run in a million different directions, baby, but no. I'm not going to get mad. There's no turning back at this point."

Another bit of hesitation came from here before she said, "Hank, Perry, and Jack."

That time it was a pause that came from me. "My best friends...my groomsmen...the same guys I went to high school with? How long have you been daydreaming about them like that?"

"See, you sound mad about it."

"I'm not, baby. I'm just obviously curious. You can't blame me."

"I have always had this fantasy since we got married. But it's not in an individual way. I just imagine the gangbang. It's not like I imagine just Jack. It's a group fantasy. I don't know how to explain it."

"So it's just a gangbang fantasy. Is it really that strong?"

She nodded in shame.

"I'm not asking you to make you feel bad and stuff, baby. I'm just trying to understand. But at the end of the day, I'm sure they'd be on board with it. They all always talk about how hot you are. It's just the whole seeing each other's penises that they'd have to get past."

"I want you to be part of it, too, you know."

How had I not thought of that? I guess I was trying my best to be selfless. "Really? I didn't think I was included for whatever reason."

"You're my husband. Of course, I'd want you to be part of it. I'd like you to oversee it, if that makes sense. You're a big part of it."

More mixed feelings came into my head. This was because I didn't know exactly how to feel. On one hand, I was completely flattered that she wanted me to be part of it. It put my mind at ease. But at the same time, the situation was what it was. At the end of the day, it was still my wife getting gangbanged. There was so much to reconcile, so much to take in.

"I appreciate that, baby. I guess I'll be part of it, if that's what you want. But we just have to make sure that this is really what you want. Because once it happens, there's no going back."

She nodded. But it was the type of nod that told me that she wanted it. She was giving me a yes to the whole situation. Carly was about to get gangbanged. And I was going to support her.

* * *

The day had come. Jack, Hank, and Perry all had agreed to do the deed. They were a little taken aback by it, obviously. But once we spoke about it, we started to joke around, and it didn't feel taboo.

The hardest part about that day was waiting for them to arrive. Carly and I sat on the couch together with the TV off. I think we both had a few jitters and rightfully so. What was about to happen was taboo, after all. I knew that there would probably be no one that I could relate to after this. It wasn't like this was a common occurrence for couples. Sure, I could always talk to my friends about it, but I had a feeling that we would probably want to after it happened. But I had no way of telling. Everything moving forward was going to be a brand-new experience. It was one that I couldn't even predict.

"Are you okay?" Carly asked me.

"You've asked me that ten times, and each time I keep telling you yes."

She nodded in confirmation. There was a little bit of shame in her, I felt. Once again, it was as though she felt like she was being a burden. And I didn't know how to pull that from her. I didn't know how to make her feel at ease with the whole situation without her thinking that I was lying.

"Baby I want you to know that everything's okay. I wouldn't have agreed to this otherwise."

"All right, I'm just making sure. I don't want to make a mistake in this marriage. I don't want to do something that's going to ruin us."

"Nothing could ever ruin us, babe."

That was when the doorbell rang. My heart started to race. I was the one that got up and answered it. With each step that I took, I lost a bit more breath. It was the strangest type of anxiety. When I opened the door, I looked at my three friends, who looked almost as uncomfortable as I did. "Let's let loose, guys."

Jack and Perry both laughed, and they all walked in. Suddenly it all felt real to me. I mean, it did feel real to me when I was on the couch, but there was something different about them all being in my home.

"Where is she?" Hank asked. "Is she all right?"

"Yeah, we just all have jitters."

They nodded. "You're doing this with us, right?" Jack asked.

"Yep. That's what she wants."

They followed me into the living room. Hank was the muscled one. Jack was tall, skinny, and had curly hair. Perry was the shortest of the group, kind of stocky, and had blonde-brown hair. Whenever I thought of my friends, I felt like I had a mix of them all. I was muscled and had dark hair, and it was curly. I also felt like it was the hairiest one out of them all. But it wasn't like Carly was going to be discovering my body. She was going to be discovering my friends' bodies.

"Hi, guys," Carly said. "You guys don't have to be uncomfortable or anything. I mean, if you are, you don't have to do this."

"If I say that I do want to do this, I don't want you, Steven, to get offended. You know what I mean?"

I appreciated that for my friend. I enjoyed the transparency. "Don't worry about it, Hank. I want you to want to do this. It's okay if you guys are turned on and find her sexy. That's why you're here."

"All right, so let's stop wasting time and let's just hit the bedroom. I'm horny." My wife saying that in front of other people was crazy. It was like we were breaking a wall down. It was also crazy to think about how many invisible walls we put up in front of ourselves on a daily basis without even realizing it.

We all followed my wife into the bedroom. Various images flashed across my mind. I guess I was kind of imagining what was going to happen. I knew that whatever I imagined was going to not even get close to what was actually going to happen. I just couldn't believe that it was going down. My friends were really about to see my wife naked. She was about to have three different cocks in her plus mine. That called for a joke. It was a joke that also had some truth in it.

"You guys are all clean of STDs and stuff, right?" I said with a jokey tone, but I meant it.

"I'm clean," Hank said first.

"Me too," Perry said.

"I have herpes," Jack joked.

"Your ass better not have herpes. You can't care about that shit."

When we were in the room, there was a very surreal feeling to it all. I didn't even know how to start. I was kind of leaving it up to my wife. It was her fantasy, so I wanted it to be accurate.

We all stood there for a moment. And then she looked at us with a smile. "I want you guys to strip me. That's how I always envisioned it."

"I've stripped her a million times. So you guys have your fun."

It was a second delay on their part. I guess no one wanted to go first out of respect for me. But then Hank would be someone that took the initiative. The other boys followed after. Hank pushed Carly down on the bed and held her down by her arms. She looked like she liked it. I walked over to watch.

"Take her pants off, boys," Hank said.

It was Perry who grabbed her yoga pants and pulled them down. There was her panties before them. I couldn't believe that a thin piece of fabric was the only thing separating her pussy from my friends.

"You want to take her panties off, Stephen?" Jack asked me.

"You do it."

She had the biggest smile on her face as she watched everyone decide what to do. Jack gained the confidence to do it, slipping his fingers underneath her thong and yanking it down.

For the first time ever, my friends were all looking down at her pussy. There was a bit of stubble there. It was the hottest thing.

I went around and took her arms from Hank. "Eat that shit out," I said to Hank.

I began to watch my friend lick her box. Jack grabbed her titty, even though she still had a shirt on. I took care of that for him. When I took her shirt off, it was Perry who unhooked her bra. Seconds later, her breasts made their debut in the room. Hank was busy eating her out. She closed her eyes in pleasure. I couldn't believe that another man was pleasuring my wife, let alone my best friend. Jack who was sucking on one of her titties. Perry took the other one. I just rubbed her face while they all had their way with her. It was like a feeding season.

While they all did that, I figured someone out of the guys had to take their clothes off. My dick was hard, and I was a little embarrassed to show my friends what it looked like but whatever. That's what we were doing. So I got naked while they all had their way with my wife.

Jack was the first one to look up from her titty and see my hard dick. "Oh shit," he said.

When he said that, both Hank and Perry looked up in the direction of where Jack was staring. All eyes were on my dick. Carly couldn't help but see what everyone was looking at. I wasn't gay, but there was something about everyone looking at my dick that turned me on. I actually wanted to feel what it felt like to have my friend's hand on my dick. I let Hank grab it. While he did that, Carly started to touch herself. I guessed that she enjoyed seeing it.

My friends were watching her jerk off. It was a hell of a sight. And then while she did that, they all started to get undressed. No longer did I feel super uncomfortable about the whole thing. We had passed that stage. We were in the thick of it now. One by one, I looked at my friends' penises. Oddly enough, the man who was the most ripped, Hank, had the smallest direct dick. Perry had the largest one, and it was kind of my size. Jack's was in between in size. I couldn't believe that I was comparing dicks with my best friends. I will say that Hank had the most veined-up one, though.

He was the first one to stick his penis inside my wife. It really didn't sink in until he was thrusting in and out of her. She didn't look like she was getting too much pleasure out of it. I wondered if she wanted Perry's dick more than my size.

Perry didn't actually last long, though. He pulled out really quickly and started to come on the floor to his hand. Hank turned her over and put her into doggy style. He fucked her like that. I took it upon myself to take my dick and stick it in her mouth while Hank was doing his business. It definitely beat just standing around.

There was something new about getting head from her while she was getting railed from behind. Jack was jerking himself off while this was all going down. He actually finished himself. Hank pulled out shortly after. It was weird seeing Hank come. I had never seen his body scrunch up the way that it had. What I noticed, though, was that Carly hadn't come yet. So I turned her over and I put my dick inside of her.

We locked eyes, and it was as though no one else was in the room with us. Somehow it was a very intimate moment. I slipped my hand behind her head. It was what I always did while we had sex. I changed up my rhythm according to the pleasure on her face, and before I knew it, she was clutching at the mattress sheets and opening her mouth wide. Her eyes shut as she finished. I pulled out after that. I didn't think I would be able to come because my friends were there. But I didn't need to. Because I knew that I had satisfied my wife. I had given her her fantasy, and I didn't feel insecure about it. I felt like I had done something incredible.

Just goes to show you that getting outside your comfort zone isn't a bad thing especially when it comes to romance. Because no matter what the circumstances were, I loved my wife.

The Reunion
By Andre Moore

"Michael." I remembered Shea saying my name when we both lost our virginity at prom. Up until that moment, my name had a different meaning. I was just Michael. I was someone's son, someone's student, someone's friend. In that bedroom with Shea that night, I was someone's lover.

So much time had passed leading up to my driving to the high school reunion. I didn't know what to expect. I didn't even know if Shea would be there. But I hoped that she was. Embarrassingly enough, she was the one part of the high school reunion that I was looking forward to. Sure, as I drove my Lincoln convertible, I knew that I was successful and had nothing to be ashamed of. I was a stockbroker. I probably had more money than most of the people attending the high school reunion, but none of that mattered to me. I didn't care about money or success like that. I cared about connections and experiences. Shea had provided me with both at the end of my high school tenure. How could I forget about a girl like that and not look forward to seeing her?

There was the school as I pulled up to it. It looked just the same as it had when I was 18 years old. The only difference was that it looked kind of smaller. They say that happens to you when you go back to the places that you knew as a kid. Well, I was there, and I hoped that the event itself didn't feel as small as the school. I was only going because my mother had given me a call and encouraged me to go. She was always fond of nostalgic events, things that would connect you to your past so that you would not forget your identity. It wasn't my old identity that I didn't like. It was the bland new one that I had. I guess I felt a little empty. I had success, but I didn't have a family. But there's no crying in baseball. It was time for me to get in there. I was 38 years old, time wasn't waiting for me.

Walking into the place, I thought of Shea once more. I thought of that night more specifically. I remembered taking her top off and seeing her breasts for the first time. I remembered the warmth of her kiss like it was my first ever kiss. Then there was her pussy. For a man who had never seen one up close and had never been allowed to touch one, it was like seeing food in the desert. Except I was a man who didn't even know what that metaphorical food tasted like at that moment. But when I tasted it, oh my God. It was a feast.

She had told me that it hurt when I had stuck my dick in her. She told me to go slow and kept asking me if she was bleeding. But she wasn't bleeding. She was just beautiful. A lot of people regret their first time. Not me. Mine was blissful. Mine could have been in some sort of romantic movie.

"Michael. You came. After 20 years you're here." My old friend Malcolm came up to me and pulled me in for a half hug and a five. "So fuckin' happy to see you in person rather than on Facebook."

"Likewise, man. Likewise. It's been too long. Life is flying by."

We both kinds of nodded at that statement. He was my literal best friend in high school. We played football together, we went home and watched games together. We got in trouble together. One time, he got into an unlocked car and drove off with me in the passenger seat. Lord knows how we didn't get locked up for carjacking. We gave the car back, of course. But man, were we in trouble.

"So how's life been for you, man?" Malcolm asked.

Suddenly my attention went elsewhere. It was no disrespect toward Malcolm, but the apple of my eye—she was there. Shea.

She had been talking to someone I didn't recognize. She looked just as beautiful as when I saw her last. She had aged perfectly. Like fine wine. Whatever she was saying to the person she was talking to, they were joking around because there was that intoxicating laugh. I related to her because she was one of the few African Americans at our school. It was me, Malcolm, and a handful of others. We knew each other's culture. We understood the world that we were in. We knew how hard things were out there. So it was nice to come back and see that she had made something of herself. She didn't have Facebook or Instagram or any of that stuff. But I could tell just by the way she carried herself that she was doing okay in life.

Malcolm had caught my eye. "Oh man, look who it is. You don't have to waste your time talking to me. I know how badly you want to go talk to her. Just tell me you haven't been waiting since high school to do this."

"She could be married for all I know."

"There's only one way to find out, Michael. I'll be here when you're done. If you don't come back, I'm proud of you."

Malcolm and I both laughed.

Walking over to Shea gave me butterflies. She looked like she was finishing up her conversation. But even while she was still talking, she looked at me, and her eyes widened. That was a good sign. I couldn't get a look at her hands. I wanted to see if there was a wedding ring on there. Either way, I was still going to talk to her.

"Hold on, I have to say hello to this man," Shea said. "Michael Johnson!"

The hug that we gave each other gave me goosebumps. I didn't want to let go. She smelled like candy and flowers. Her touch was gentle, welcoming, and just as I remembered.

"How the hell have you been, Michael?"

"I've been good. Better now."

I still couldn't get a look at her hand. The way it was positioned, her cup was hiding the ring finger. I was also trying not to be obvious about it.

She smiled at my comment. "I can't believe we're

here after all this time. Did the school seem smaller to you when you–"

"Yes!" I laughed. "Sorry to cut you off, I just thought I was the only one. Oddly enough standing here with you, though, nothing feels small about this moment. Is that too cheesy?"

I made her laugh with that comment. She put her empty glass down, and I finally saw that she was ringless. "That's not cheesy at all." Her eyes drifted to my hand. We caught each other.

"You know I'm going to have to call you out on that, right?"

"What? Me looking at your hand to see if you're married? That's just an observation. It's nice to know someone's circumstances. I don't want your wife to think that I'm flirting with you, you know?"

There were butterflies in my chest once more. Just the word *flirting* made me feel like we were back in a day together. "Well, Shea, you don't have to worry about my wife caring about something like that cuz it's just you and me."

She laughed. "From the looks of it, there's about a hundred other people here. It's not just you and me."

I wasn't sure if I should be bold, but I also knew that again, time wasn't going to wait for me. "How do we make it so that it's you and me?"

"The auditorium."

I smiled. We both looked around for a moment and then at the exit. No one was guarding it, and no one was paying attention to us. So we made for that exit. And once we were through it, my butterflies started to throw a party.

"Holy shit, Michael, are we about to do this?"

"You're right. We won't do this. I don't want to upset your husband."

She found that funny and kissed me. Time stopped when her lips touched mine. As much as I wanted to continue kissing her, I pulled off and said, "We can't do this here. Let's keep going."

We continued to walk down the hallway, made a left, and we were in the auditorium. There were some lights on, but it was pretty dim. Walking down the seating area, we went to the stage and then went behind it. No one was going to find us. Finally, we could continue.

I went right back to kissing her, pinning her arms against the wall and letting my years of sexual frustration toward her get unleashed.

"Why did we drift apart, Michael?" she asked through kisses.

"I joined the military. Remember? You didn't wait for me."

"I'm sorry."

"It's in the past." I put my tongue in her mouth, and she put hers in mine. It was like we were having a sexual sword fight. I missed her so much that I wanted to cry. The way that she was kissing me I kind of felt like she was going through the same palette of emotions. And that warmed my heart.

"I don't ever want to let you go again. I don't know if you feel the same way," I said to her. "But I need this."

She didn't say anything back to me, but that didn't matter because I knew that in the heat of the moment words weren't necessary.

I let my hands fall to her breasts. She was in a tank top and yoga pants. But those weren't going to be on for long. Her breasts felt a little bigger than the last time I'd held them. Or maybe it was just so long ago that I didn't remember. I just knew that I would never forget touching them that time. I could feel her nipples through her bra. I couldn't wait any longer, so I lifted the tank top off and unhooked her bra. Out sprung her double-D titties. They were just as I remembered them. Charcoal-colored nipples so big that they almost covered the entire front of her breast. I wasted no time putting them in my mouth.

Well, I put at least one in my mouth. The other one I continued to squeeze.

Her hand went low. She began to jerk me with my pants on. She had no trouble finding my dick because I was rock solid. My dick was screaming to get out once it was bent down while it was hard. It was so uncomfortable, yet every time that she jerked it, it felt amazing. Call me crazy, but the way that she was doing it was the same way that she did it the night that we lost our virginity. It was like she remembered. Gentle, then rough, teasing, then rough. She remembered how I liked it. But I also remembered how she liked it. Was I going to stick my hand down her yoga pants and feel that wet pussy of hers? For so many years, I'd thought of her. For so many years, I'd imagined that night over and over again. And there it was. There she was. None of it made sense to me. But in times like that, you don't question it.

The hand that I was squeezing her breast with, I brought down to her yoga pants and slipped it underneath. I could feel the lace of her panties—the last barrier between my fingers and her pussy.

My fingers went. The warmth and wetness of her pussy drove me insane. Her little clitoris was on the tips of my fingers. Her mouth opened, and then her eyes closed shut as I maneuvered my way around there. There was no greater feeling.

While I was doing that, she opened her eyes and looked at me for a second almost as if she had realized what she wanted. She ran her hand behind the back of my head and pulled me in for an aggressive kiss. I say aggressive because it was passionate but with a little extra. There was that emotion that I had inside of me being displayed on her. I knew what she was feeling. She missed me just as I had missed her. That was validation.

With validation comes more passion. I bent down and yanked her yoga pants off. She stepped out of them, leaving herself and her thong. "My bad, I probably shouldn't be getting you naked."

"I don't give a fuck."

She was the one that pulled her underwear off. My eyes fell to her pussy. There was a little bit of coarse black hair covering her opening. The last time I saw it, it was completely shaved. I liked it better than the new way.

I took my pants off along with my boxers. My dick was saluting her hard.

"Fuck me, Michael."

She didn't have to ask me twice. Bending her over, I spread her cheeks and pounded my dick right into her hole. I looked at her little butthole while I thrust in and out. We had it done in doggy when we lost our virginity. This was the first time I was seeing her butthole. I ran my finger over it and she didn't flinch or anything. She was holding on to a bar that was attached to the wall; it looked like some sort of handrail. She had one hand over her mouth to muffle her sounds. She was getting louder with each thrust. That was turning me on more every time I heard it.

She was making noises that I had never heard before. They were these light little moans. Muffled moans, of course.

With each thrust that I gave her, I pulled her hips toward me. I held on to her like I was on a roller coaster. Her ass was making waves each time my dick went inside her. When I would pull my dick out, I'd see a little bit of cream lining the rim.

The site turned me on to the point where I was close to finishing. As much as I wanted to continue railing against her, I needed that big finale. I noticed that she was clutching the bar just a little bit harder. Her body had stopped moving for a second, and then she covered her mouth a lot harder than she had been. She had finished.

I gave her maybe six more pumps, but I had to pull out immediately after that. I came into my hands. She watched me come. It made me come harder to know that she was looking at me.

We both freshened up in a nearby bathroom. And when we came out, we looked as though we were in our senior year of high school all over again. Despite our dark complexions, we had red in our cheeks because of our embarrassment. It was a good type of embarrassment, though.

"Did we just do that?" Shea asked me as if I hadn't been there.

"Yes, we did. And I don't regret it one bit. Your body looked great."

She gave me a little smack on the shoulder. "Stop it. You're more of a pig now."

"Can you blame me after that? To be honest, I've been thinking about you for years."

She leaned up against the bar and gave me compassionate eyes. "Then why didn't you ever reach out? Why did you wait for so long?"

I shrugged and leaned on the bar next to her. "I don't know. When I got out of the military, things got hectic and I needed to look for work, and I thought you moved on. Your lack of social media didn't allow me to creep you, you know. A girl like you, I figured you were going to be happy with me in the picture or not. A girl like you doesn't wait around for a guy like me."

"That's where you're wrong, Michael. Because just as you were thinking about me for all these years, I was thinking about you, too. I missed you, Michael. I came to this stupid reunion 20 years later because I wanted you to be here. And here you are. We have quite the love story because look, we both wanted each other."

"It seems like we wasted a lot of our lives. We could have been doing this a lot sooner."

"Well, I wouldn't necessarily want to only do this in the back of an auditorium. I think we should get dinner sometime. We should start seeing if we still work. We know sexually that we do. But now the rest has to fall into place."

"I would like that, Shea. I would like that."

We held each other's hands at that moment.

Only time would tell whether or not our love from high school carried over and passed the lust that we still had. It was one thing to have sex in an auditorium in secret after missing each other for so long. But I had a feeling that our love would endure. I had this gut instinct that if we had been thinking about each other for that long, there had to be a payoff.

Never did I think that my life would have taken a

turn in the way that it did. I always thought that the girl who I loved for so many years would have moved on, and we would just be a distant memory that I would have to replay over and over and over again. Because I even did that when I dated other girls.

So what is love exactly? It's a thing that waits even when time doesn't want to. I'd like to think that love is more powerful than time. Love is absolutely everything.

Three's Not a Crowd
By J. Martino

It had been a while since Amy and Jack had someone watch the baby. That day, it was his mother-in-law. She had agreed to babysit while Amy's sister, Grace, was en route to come over to the house.

Grace was coming over to do Amy's hair so that Jack and Amy could go to a wedding the next day. They would be gone the entire weekend. Jack had one problem, though: He found Amy's sister to be incredibly attractive.

He thought about how she was only 20 minutes away. He had jitters. It wasn't that he didn't love Amy; he loved her with all his heart. She was his wife, his everything, his more than everything. But at the same time, he did have an attraction to her sister. Grace was funny, intelligent, see how to charm her, a nerdy charm. And yet she wasn't a nerd at all. She was beautiful. She had freckles on her cheek, reddish hair, curves in all the right places, and he knew that she'd caught him checking out her ass a few times but had never dared to bring it up. This would be the first time Grace was over at his place with just him and his wife. He knew nothing would come of it. It wasn't like they were going to have sex or anything like that, but just knowing that she was coming over sent him into a fantasy world. Would his wife ever be okay with a fantasy world like that? Would she ever understand the urge that he had for her sister? While still loving her? Those were questions that he would never dare to ask her.

"She's ten minutes away," Amy said while pouring herself a glass of iced tea. "Oh, by the way, she and Sean broke up. I mean, we all saw it coming, but it's official now."

Sean was the on-and-off boyfriend who he was friends with and also envied. "Oh damn," Jack said. "Yeah, I mean I saw it coming, but I didn't think it would be this soon. How is she taking it?"

"She's doing good. I think she wasn't surprised by them breaking up either."

For whatever reason, Jack saw that as an opportunity to test the waters for how he saw her sister.

They had an open relationship in terms of communi-
cation. They could talk about anything, so maybe she
wouldn't be so offended if he went about things the
right way. "She's smart and funny, she'll find another
boyfriend soon." He'd almost said *pretty*. But that felt
like it was pushing it.

"Yeah. She just needs to take her time. And not
rush into anything."

He couldn't do it. He sat down at the dining
room table after they walked into the room together
and decided that there was going to be no testing of
the waters. He didn't want to ruin his entire marriage
with one comment.

"You know, I think she's prettier than me," Amy
said. She took a sip of her iced tea after saying it.

There was his opportunity. Of course, he would
never say that she was prettier because she wasn't.
She was pretty in her own way. She was different
from Amy. Amy had blond hair, cute little lips, wide
brown eyes, a rack to die for, and her version of
charm. So now how would he say that he found
Grace attractive without putting her down?

"I don't think she's prettier than you. I think
you're both very pretty. You're both very pretty in
your ways."

"So you think she's really pretty?"

"I do. But I love you." He was going to stop there, even though he felt like he needed to say more. Less was more.

"If we weren't married, would you date her?"

He knew the answer, but he also knew he couldn't just say that to her. He had to make it kind of difficult. There was a fine line between the truth that she wanted to hear and the truth that she needed to hear. "Come on, babe. I love you. We're together, so the question is irrelevant."

She cut her eyes at Jack but had a smirk on her face as if it was all playful to her. "So you would have sex with her if we weren't married. That's what I'm getting from this."

Jack pretended that he was frustrated and then said, "If you must know, yes. If you didn't exist and we weren't married, yeah, I would take Grace out."

"Would you have sex with her?"

"Do I have to say these things?"

"Oh my God, so you would."

"You're forcing me to say these things, Amy. I never said any of this."

She gave Jack a long look as if he just needed to fess up. "All right, yeah, I would have sex with her. I think she's sexy sometimes. But again, I love you. I don't want you to be offended by any of that. I think some women are pretty, that's all. That doesn't mean that I would cheat on you."

Amy chuckled. "Fair enough. But okay, what if I had approached you about having a threesome or something, would you do that?"

"Threesome with your sister? Isn't that incest?"

"She's my step-sister."

Jack chuckled. "Right. I mean, I look at her as your sister, so I mean I thought you would look at her as your sister like that. Like blood."

"Can you just be honest with me and stop jumping around the question? I know she's my step-sister, and I know how I grew up with her and everything. I'm not trying to clarify any of that, I just want to get answers out of you."

His cheeks went completely red. "Babe, you know Grace is going to be here soon. And this is what we're talking about."

"Yeah, so hurry up and say what you need to say. If I approached you about having a threesome with me and my sister, would you do it?"

"Yes, babe. I would have a threesome with both of you. Now can we drop it?"

The doorbell rang. Before Amy got up from the table, she gave Jack another long look. But there was no maliciousness in there. This surprised him. He thought she would have taken it a lot worse because in the past she had been jealous. But it seemed when it came to the subject that they were on, she was just more intrigued than anything.

When Amy let Grace in, there was an awkwardness that fell upon Jack. It probably wasn't anything that Grace noticed, but he noticed it within himself. "Hey, Grace," he forced out to try to combat the feelings that he had inside himself. Pushing forward always helped in awkward situations.

"Hey, guys," Grace said while she stepped in.

Amy was quieter than normal. It was only when she said, "All right, I guess we should start on my hair and get this over with" that Jack knew she wasn't going to drop what he just said. Finally, he felt like he had done something wrong even though she had goaded him into saying what he said.

"You all right?" Grace asked Amy.

Jack made sure that he stayed quiet. He didn't want to be involved, even though he already was.

When they got into the living room, Amy replied, "Yeah, I'm good. Just have a bit of a headache. How's everything with you?"

They started to chit chat, and Jack thought about the prospect of having a threesome with them both. He couldn't believe that he had been talking about it.

He also couldn't believe that it was finally out in the open that he found Grace attractive. Even while they were talking, he peeped at her cleavage. She was in a hoodie, and underneath was a tank top. But the tank top did nothing to hide her breasts. Part of him wished that the conversation had gone further than it had.

When they were done chatting, Grace started to take all her hair equipment out. Jack took a seat on the couch and flipped on the TV. He put football on so he could remain distracted while that giant ass on Grace stood in the room before his wife. His eyes ventured there by mistake, and Amy caught it.

"I saw that," she said.

Jack's cheeks went red as Grace looked at them both in confusion.

"What did you see, Amy? Why are you being annoying today?" He said the last sentence out of nerves. He couldn't believe that the entire situation was happening.

"I'm being annoying? You're the one who wants to fuck my sister."

"Um, what?" Grace asked. It looked as though her cheeks were going red too.

Jack had to decide whether or not he was going to elaborate on the situation to Grace. He didn't want to because he knew how awkward she would feel. But, despite Amy, he was going to call out the elephant in the room. "Fine, Amy, since you had to bring this up. Grace, Amy, and I were talking and she asked me if I thought you were pretty and stuff. I said I did and then she asked if I would ever have a threesome with you both out of curiosity. Not that she was throwing it out there, but I said yeah I would. I also said that I would date you if she didn't exist. And now she's all salty. I just want to throw it out here that I love Amy, and just because I find someone pretty doesn't mean that I'm going to cheat on her or something okay? I hope you don't feel too awkward now, Grace, but you can blame your sister."

Grace's cheeks were redder than Jack's. He found it cute. He also was turned on by the fact that all of his personal information was out there for the first time in six years. "I don't know what to say to all that," Grace said. "That's quite a discussion. I would only ever have a threesome if Amy okayed it."

Amy let her mouth fall open, and Grace laughed. "You would fuck my husband?"

"Not behind your back. Only if you were involved. I would never encourage cheating or anything like that. I just, I don't know. Do you know what I mean? It's a weird thing."

"So do you find Jack attractive?"

Grace shrugged, and Jack knew why. She just didn't want to upset Amy anymore.

"Amy, I think you're taking this all the wrong way. I'm in love with you. And she's your sister. She would never do anything to hurt you, you know what I'm saying? We just I guess find one another attractive without it being harmful. I'm not trying to speak for Grace—"

"No, he's saying it right," Grace added. "Jack isn't an ugly man, like if Amy came to me and said you want to have a threesome, I'd be okay with it. It's not like I'm sitting around thinking about it, but I would do it."

Amy stayed quiet for a moment as Grace began her hair. But Amy shot out of her chair and stopped Grace from doing it. Jack quickly analyzed her mood; she didn't seem angry, she seemed more energetic. "All right, so then let's all have a threesome. If everyone's on board with it, then why don't we just get it out of the way?"

Both Grace and Jack laughed, but it was out of nerves. "I think you're losing your mind, Amy."

She simmered down for a moment. And then she said, "All right, maybe I'm interested in it now."

"Really?" Grace asked.

"Yeah, I don't know. I would never have a three-some with anyone else, and now I'm intrigued."

Jack imagined his wife's pussy getting wet. He knew what she meant by intrigued. She meant turned on.

It was Grace who laughed at that. Jack wanted to see her reaction to it all. Jack had had sex with Amy a million times. It was the prospect of seeing her naked in front of her sister that turned him on too. But with the prospect of actually having sex with her sister while she was there, Jack needed to know what Grace's opinion on that would be. He needed to know if this was going to happen. Or if there was a chance of it happening.

"I mean, I'm down for it. But only if you're cool with it," she said to her sister. "I want to preface by saying I would never do anything to hurt you or betray you or anything like that. You know what I mean."

"So you find Jack attractive?"

Grace shrugged. "I don't want to get in trouble." She laughed. "You know what I mean? I don't want to upset you."

This time, it was Amy who laughed. Jack guessed she hadn't been as sensitive as he had thought. "You're not upsetting me. I'm the one that's bringing it all up. So if we all want to do this, then let's do this. Screw it."

Grace and Jack looked at one another. Butterflies didn't begin to explain what was going on in his chest at that moment. He couldn't believe it was happening. It almost felt like a prank. "If you both are on board, I'm on board," he said. "But again, I'm not going to do this if it ruins things."

"I don't think it'll ruin things. It'll be our inside thing."

Grace put her hair equipment down, and that's how he knew things were about to happen. "So how do we start a threesome? I've never been in one."

"Let's go to the bedroom," Amy said.

They both followed her, and Jack's breath was rapid. He had to calm himself down because he wanted to enjoy what was about to happen. He was so excited. His dick was beginning to get hard as they walked.

When they got to the bedroom, Jack finally calmed his nerves and allowed himself to finally look at Grace as she looked at him. He also noticed Amy looking at them both.

"You're looking at her ass?"

"I am looking at her ass."

Grace's cheeks went red. "I can't believe we're about to do this."

Amy didn't say anything, so he said, "I know this is crazy. All right, I guess both of you get naked first. And then I'll get naked."

They both laughed. "Why do you get to get naked last?" Amy asked.

"Because I'm the dude."

Amy shook her head and started to take her clothes off. "I'll get naked first, then Grace, then you. We'll all get acquainted with one another."

Grace laughed, and it was cute. Jack stole glances at Grace as she watched her sister get undressed. It was one of the hottest sights. Amy took off her top and stood there for a moment in her jeans and bra. They were seconds away from seeing her breasts.

Amy slipped her fingers behind her back and unhooked her bra. This would be the first time that her sister had ever seen her breasts. And then they were out in the room. Her little pink nipples said hello to everyone.

"One's bigger than the other," Grace joked.

Jack got bold and stuck one of them in his mouth.

"Oh my God," Grace said as she watched him do it. It was crazy to be sexual in front of Grace. It was crazy to have her see him put a nipple in his mouth. It was like an alternate reality.

Jack let go, and Amy took off her pants. Seconds after that, her panties were off. Amy did this little gesture as if to say *Here I am.* "This is me. I'm naked."

"Touch her titties," Jack asked Grace.

There was a little bit of hesitation on Grace's part, but after a second or so, Jack watched her hand go to her sister's titties. She squeezed them. Surprisingly, she also gave them a suck. He couldn't believe it. She sucked it for a long time. Amy even put her hand on Grace's head for a bit.

"Grace!" Amy blurted out.

Jack wasn't sure if it was appropriate to touch his dick, but he sure did want to.

"All right, my turn," Grace said before she lifted her tank top. Jack's heart rate increased.

Grace stood in her bra and yoga pants. She took off her yoga pants next. A bit of her belly flopped out, but it only complimented her curves. The next thing she took off was her bra. She had bigger nipples than Amy, and they were pierced. Jack got bold yet again and grabbed one. She took her panties off and had a little bit of a ginger bush. Jack went to touch her pussy, and she allowed it.

"How come you're not touching my pussy?" Amy asked.

He took his other hand and touched her pussy as well. "I can't believe this is happening."

He moved both his hands and undid his pants after taking his shirt off. It was Grace who looked at him while he unzipped. She was seconds away from seeing his dick for the first time. Six years they had known one another. For six years, he'd had to stifle his sexual urges for her.

After six years, his hard dick flopped into the room. Amy grabbed it. Grace kissed him. He had a feeling that he was not going to last long during the threesome. But he was going to try his best.

Everyone was naked. Amy and Grace pushed him onto the bed. Amy continued to stroke his dick while he lay there. Grace stuck her tongue in his mouth. He put one hand on her face and then ran his fingers through her hair. Amy started to suck his dick. Jack moved his hand down to Grace's pussy and started to jerk her off. It was everything that he had imagined. Her little clitoris was wet, and her body soon started to become like an instrument in his grasp.

He moved his other hand to start jerking Amy off as she moved up closer to him. Both the sisters let out these little cute moans at the same time. It was a dreamland for Jack.

Amy continued to put her lips on Jack's dick, and Grace went down there too. They both started to lick his rod up and down.

"You guys are going to have to stop, I'm going to come."

Grace started to laugh. "You wanted this, and you can't even handle it."

"Let's make his ass come," Amy said.

"Hold on." Grace took her sister and laid her down next to Jack.

"What are you doing, Grace?"

Grace spread Amy's legs open and started to eat her out.

"Grace! Oh my God, Grace."

Jack stroked his dick as she licked his wife in the most sensitive of areas. It was crazy to think that she knew how her sister tasted. She knew what she was like sexually now.

Jack hadn't expected it, but a few minutes later, he recognized the signs in his wife. She was coming. Her body contorted upward, and she stiffened. And when she was done, taking a deep breath, Grace said, "Mission accomplished part one." She laughed.

The next great state was to get on Jack in cowgirl

style. It only took Jack a few seconds before he had to push her massive ass off of his dick. While he finished, he couldn't believe that he had seen that ass without anything covering it. He couldn't believe that he had seen her holes and watched his wife getting eaten out by her sister.

It was a threesome that he would never forget. None of them would ever forget it. It was their secret, and maybe one day, they would do it again.

.

A Snack Before Dinner
By Kellan Fitz

Love was a complicated thing. It only becomes complicated when you want something and you haven't gotten it. For me, I just wanted my wife to let me cum in her mouth.

We had been married for four years. And Amanda had been pretty much open to everything. We tried anal once, but she didn't like it. But we still tried it. And I appreciate that. And I thought that I would be satisfied with just trying it and calling it a day. But when you're with someone for so long, so many years, you start to wonder about things. You start to have these fantasies that you never thought you'd have or care about. And I don't know, something about coming in her mouth was driving me up a wall.

"There's a new *America's Got Talent* tonight, Jeff," Amanda said to me while she made dinner.

"Oh, great. We can watch that while we eat."

"Yep."

As you can see from our dialogue, we have a pretty simple life. We have been trying to have a baby for a while, so we did everything in our power to not obsess over that. And that meant focusing on us. It meant loving each other with our full hearts. But while waiting for a baby, the mind still had its curiosities. The problem here was how did I bring up such a dirty thing to her. Amanda was the furthest thing from a prude, but it would still feel raunchy to me to bring that type of stuff up to her. I always wanted to respect Amanda.

I watched her cook. She was in this skimpy little underwear, a tank top, and her flip-flops. She had wide hips that were beautiful. She was so impressive that it almost looked fake, but they couldn't have been more real. I loved every single bit of her. It was one of those things where I could try to find the flaw, and it would take me years to do that. It sounded cheesy, but after being married to her for four years, I saw it as an accomplishment. We loved each other so much, and a lot of people couldn't say that about their marriage.

"You're quiet, what's up?" Amanda asked me. I mean I guess if I had to really find something that I didn't like about her, it would be that she never let me rest in silence. If there was something wrong with me, she knew. She saw right through me like she had an x-ray machine in her eyes.

"Babe, I'm good."

She left her spoon in the pan and turned around. "What's bothering you? I know something's bothering you."

Well, at that point I knew that I couldn't hide it from her anymore. It was just a matter of how I was going to say it. Again, I didn't want to be raunchy. I didn't want to make her uncomfortable. And I also didn't want to put her in a position where she felt pressured. Of course, she would never do anything that she didn't want to do, but just mentioning it could make her feel guilty. "I was just thinking about sex stuff."

She raised an eyebrow with her hands on her hips. "Sex stuff? What type of sex stuff?"

I looked down at the floor, and my cheeks grew a little red. It was funny how you could have sex with a woman for many years and still get a little bashful in front of her. It was like how I still couldn't poop in front of her. "I don't know, I don't want to make you uncomfortable."

"Babe, we're married. You've seen my period pad. You've seen me queef. Just tell me."

"All right. I guess I want you to let me finish in your mouth."

She stared at me. It was a long stare as if she couldn't believe what I had just said. Or maybe it was because she was shocked that I was bringing it up again. I'd brought it up in passing before but nothing serious. So I guess the fact that I was serious about it led her to stare at me a little bit longer. I had no idea; that was just my assumption. Even though I had been with my wife for a very long time, it was still on what was on my mind at the end of the day. "You mean you want to cum in my mouth?"

I nodded. Something about nodding felt to me like I was more certain about it.

"I mean, I don't know." She turned back around to start cooking. That was how I knew that I probably wasn't going to ever get that. If she was uncomfortable with it, I wasn't going to force it.

"All right, no worries. Forget I brought it up."

She turned back around after putting her spoon back into the pan. "Is that something you really want?"

"I've been thinking about it all the time. I don't want to put pressure on you, though. If it's something that grosses you out–"

"It doesn't gross me out. I'm just scared of gagging. Like I don't know how I'm going to react to you squirting in my mouth. What if it shoots to the back of my throat and I start to throw up?"

I didn't know why, but I kind of wanted to laugh at that sentence. "I mean, again, you don't have to do this. But I felt like that when it happened. I feel like there would be some level of control there. I could be wrong, though."

She went back to cooking, not saying a word. Even though she didn't say anything, I knew that it was on her mind. It wasn't going to leave her mind because like I had tried to avoid it, she was probably feeling bad about it. And that meant that I had to step in.

I left the kitchen table and walked up to her, wrapping my arms around her waist and giving her a tight hug. "Baby, I don't want you to stress any of this, okay? You're too good to stress things like that. I don't need to come in your mouth to be satisfied in this marriage, okay? It was just a fleeting thought, that's all. Don't even give it any time of day."

"You're my husband," she said while cooking. "I

want to be able to please you. I don't want to leave anything on the table, you know." She put the spoon down and looked at me. "I'll do it."

My heart started to race. "Really?"

She turned the stove off. That was how I knew she was serious. "Let's go."

"Baby, we don't really have to do this. I don't want to make you do something that you don't want to do."

She turned around and smiled at me. The next thing that she did was put her hands on my belt buckle. I couldn't believe that this was going to happen. She was really going to suck my dick and let me come in her mouth. I almost had to pinch myself because it felt like a dream. "Let's do this."

Before I knew it, she was unbuckling my pants. Goosebumps covered my arms and the rest of my body. I was so excited that I was afraid I wouldn't be able to get it up. When you have the pressure to come into someone's mouth, it becomes a whole different game.

She pushed me into the living room while unzipping me. When I plop down on the couch, she pulled my pants down completely with my boxers. My dick was hard. I was wrong: I had no problem getting it up.

"Look at you, all veiny and shit." She giggled.

Before I could say anything, she wrapped her lips around my cock. She kept her index finger and thumb wrapped around the base. It was like she was holding a microphone. Instead of singing into it, she was sucking the life out of it. I could feel every inch of her tongue. I wasn't sure if I felt more sensitive because I knew what was coming. There was something so taboo about the whole experience for me. It felt like my wife was crossing this barrier. It was almost like she was becoming a whole different woman. I was there for it. I was ready to see her reaction when my fluids came into her mouth.

Of course, she had tasted pre-cum before, but I guess it was different for her. I guess it was a whole different experience. And in many ways, it was. I was about to know what that experience was like because I was getting closer and closer.

I could see her smiling while sucking me off. Because she probably knew that I was going to close her as well. Whenever she was sucking my dick, she could always somehow tell when I was about to climax. From what she had told me in the past it was because my dick would swell even more. I would just get so hard. And that's what was happening to me as she sucked me off.

It was pure euphoria. Unlike other times when things were kind of predictable, there was this other build-up involved. It was all because I knew what was coming. I knew that for the first time in our marriage, I was going to experience something that I had been dreaming about for years. There was, of course, the possibility that I would start to come, and she would pull right off. Maybe she would spit it out. From the way she was moving her head on my cock, I really didn't see that in the cards.

She started to suck a little bit more gently, and that's why I began to lose it. "I'm getting closer, babe," I warned her because I wanted to give her the chance to back out. Again, I didn't want her to do anything that she was uncomfortable with. I wanted to make sure she had a choice.

But her lips stayed on, and she continued to suck.

"It's going to happen, babe," I told her.

Her lips still remained.

My dick tightened. I felt the beginning stages of orgasm. It was going to be a big one. I felt bad for her because my seven inches were about to fill her mouth.

Finally, my whole body clenched up, but I kept

my eyes open. When I looked down, her lips were wrapped around my cock as I came. I just kept coming. And she didn't move. Her eyes were closed, she didn't seem uncomfortable, and when I was finished, she took her lips off and swallowed.

She looked at me. We had this moment of connection. I didn't even know what to say to her really. "That wasn't that bad. If you swallow it quickly, you don't taste anything."

I smiled. "Can't believe you just did that."

"I can't believe I just did that either."

We locked eyes again. It was as though we had transcended into a different world. There was a bond that we would always share. I had no idea what it was, but it was probably because swallowing my jizz was an intimate thing. She had been the only woman to do it. And I was happy about that. I was happy that the woman I was going to spend my entire life with had crossed that barrier and done that for me.

"I love you, babe," I told her. "You didn't have to do that, but I really love you. You don't know how much it means to me."

"I will do anything for you, baby. Now I guess I should finish dinner. I got to put something else in my mouth to wash the taste away."

We both laughed. I couldn't wait till she did it again. Because I knew that she would.

.

The Other Traditional Tenth Anniversary Gift

By Porter Lee

Ten years. Ten years to the day I had been married to Veronica. Our anniversary felt right. We had come a long way from the days when we used to argue about petty things. Now I couldn't imagine arguing with her. I wouldn't even know what we would argue about. As I sat across from her at a place called Italianissimo, I thought about how far we had come. I appreciated her in a way that she would never really realize. We had almost come to breaking up the year before we got married, and yet there we were. We were sitting across from each other, she was eating linguine, and I was having spaghetti. We were so similar yet so much the same. We thought that our cultures would have screwed us up somehow. She came from a black family, and I came from the whitest family on Long

Island. On paper, we didn't work out. And that wasn't just because of our backgrounds, but it was because of our personalities. She was into a different kind of music than me. She was outgoing, and I was introverted. She liked to party; I liked to read. But somehow, we had made it to our wedding day, and ever since then, we had no issues. It was miraculous.

"I still can't believe we're on to ten years, Michael. Remember when we almost broke up?"

"I was just thinking about that."

She had this look on her face when I said that, almost as if she didn't want to be thinking about what she'd just brought up. So now it was my job to make her feel better.

"I know it's hard to think about, that none of this would have happened if we had broken up. But we don't have to think about that anymore cuz look at us. A decade."

"What was it even over?"

I had to wrack my brain just a little bit. "I didn't have enough money for the wedding and you wanted a dessert table and I said we don't need a dessert table and then I think that was the first time that you and I yelled at each other. Before that, we hadn't blown up to that level of anger."

Veronica laughed. "You're right. We never did get mad at each other before that and even after it, we never did again. It was like we scared each other out of yelling."

I liked that analogy. It made me feel better about things. "I think it worked out for the best. We had one major blowout, and for ten more years, we haven't done it since. That's a nice record to have."

Veronica nodded and shoveled some pasta into her mouth. Even after so much time together, I still found little things about her tremendously sexy. Like the way her lips puffed out while eating her pasta. They reminded me of when she would suck my dick. "Do you remember how we celebrated five years ago?"

Five years ago was a long time for me to recall what we had done on that specific day. I couldn't remember whether it was dinner or a movie.

"I'm not talking about the date if you're trying to figure out what we did that night. I'm talking about the other stuff."

The other stuff. That was easy to remember. I brought my voice down to a whisper and said, "The night that I made you first do anal?"

She laughed and nodded her head yes. "You

didn't make me do it. I gave you consent. Did you ever think we'd be doing it for five years after that?"

"No, I thought it was going to be one and done. But you liked the little naughty girl."

Her cheeks went red, and she did her best to hide how embarrassed she was by stuffing her face with more pasta. I knew my wife. She didn't get embarrassed often, but when she did, it was fuckin' adorable. "I do like it. I never thought that I would, but I do. Remember I always used to say things shouldn't go in the butt. And now look."

"Should we be talking about this at dinner in a fancy Italian restaurant?"

"Where else should we talk about it? It's a big part of our marriage. You still like sex, right?"

I rolled my eyes at her joke. "You're still crazy after all these years."

"I'm crazy for talking about our sex life? I have an idea for this tenth anniversary."

My heart started to race. It wasn't often just like her tendency to get embarrassed that she came up with ideas like this. You know, where she would announce that she had an idea. "Oh yeah? I would love to hear this."

She wore a smirk. And then her wide brown eyes looked at mine. "You know how we celebrated our five-year? I was thinking maybe we could similarly celebrate our ten-year."

That time I smiled. Because I was always up for some anal. It was a sexual activity that never got boring. "Oh? I'm down for that. Maybe I'll even eat your ass out tonight."

She still had the smirk on her face, but she was oddly quiet. Something was up. She wasn't telling me the full story.

"What is it, Veronica? What are you holding back?"

She paused for a moment, and then revealed, "I wasn't talking about my butt."

As the shock filled me, I brought my voice down to a whisper once more. "Pegging? You want to do pegging?"

She lifted a little bag that came from a sex shop that we frequented. I knew exactly what was in that bag without her having to show me.

"Oh my God, you're serious. Can we talk about this in the car and not at dinner right now?"

"Yes or no?"

I pursed my lips and gave her a bit of a stare. I couldn't believe that we were having this discussion at dinner. I was paying a pretty penny for this dinner, and we were talking about naughty things. It was taking my focus right off my meal. "Yes. But again, can we be a little romantic at dinner and focus on this later?"

She brought her voice down to a whisper and leaned over the table. "You mentioned that you wanted this once. And now that I'm really curious, you seem to be against it."

I shrugged. "I'm not against it, baby. I guess I'm just a little nervous about it. I've never done it before. I want to; I just have the jitters. But I want to."

She smiled, and it made me feel like I was the submissive one. "All right. We'll talk about this in the car then. You don't have to do anything that's going to make you nervous or anything, but I'm ready."

Even though I said that we were going to talk about it in the car, I continued to think about what was going to happen while we were at dinner. How could I not? It was a pretty big deal. I had been thinking about getting pegged for a long time. It all started when I did anal with her. I had kind of fingered myself while masturbating one time, and it felt really good. That snowballed into thinking about other things.

When we got into the car, she wasted no time in bringing it all up. "So what makes you nervous about pegging?"

I laughed at how impatient she was. "I don't know. I've had things come out of my ass, but I rarely ever put anything up there. I'm going to have a few jitters. You're going to stick a dildo up my ass. How big is the thing?"

She reached inside the bag and yanked the dildo out - a long, veiny black dildo. "I got it in black so you would think of me."

I laughed at that. "Once again you confirm that you're crazy."

After a few seconds, she said, "I can't wait to stick this shit in you. I can't wait to feel what it feels like to fuck you instead."

My dick was getting harder with every word that she uttered. We were a few miles away from home, and suddenly, I was filled with excitement. Sure, I still had those nervous jitters overdoing it for the first time, but I was far more excited than I was nervous.

"I also got lube, of course. We were out," she continued, knowing that someone had to fill the silence. My mind was too focused on everything to talk. "Come on, you're not so nervous that you're going to be silent on me?"

"I'm not nervous, I'm just anticipating it. It's a big deal. My wife is about to fuck me in the ass. That's a big milestone."

She leaned over and adjusted her seat belt so that she could kiss me on the cheek. I found that sweet. "You're going to get fucked good, boy."

I laughed. For the rest of the ride, we listened to music on the radio. I imagined her strapping that dildo on and sticking it right in my ass. I wish I had shaved for her, but I knew she didn't care. I just couldn't believe that she was going to be looking at my asshole. We had been married for ten years, yet it still felt so personal. You kind of felt like we were going on a first date all over again. You know, right before you see someone naked for the first time. That's how it felt in the car.

Even when we got home, it was like I was entering a different house. It was like a sex house. I had these eternal goosebumps that wouldn't go away. I didn't want them to go away. I was feeling good. Now and then, Veronica and I would look at one another, and we'd have this intimate gaze where we didn't necessarily need to say anything; we both knew what was going to happen.

When we were in the bedroom, and she was laying out the stuff on the bed, she stopped for a moment as I stood there in just my pajama pants and gave me this long and warm kiss. It was the type of kiss that again felt like we had just started dating all over again. Romantic wasn't a strong enough word for it.

"You don't have to do this if you don't want to."

"I want to have a baby," I told her and brought my hand to her face. I pulled her in for another kiss, and she gave me a little bit of tongue. She had a night-gown on. I grabbed a hold of those spaghetti straps and pulled the thing down. It went from me looking at her hard nipples through the nightgown to seeing them before me. They never got old. I could stare at those things for fifty more years and still look at them like they were new. My eyes glanced down at her pussy. That was the location of where the dildo would be strapped on. I went to the bed and grabbed it to do the honors.

"Why do you feel like you're more in control when you're strapping it on me?" Veronica joked.

"I don't think it's emasculating to be fucked in the ass by my wife. It's just the feeling of it, that's all. I don't know what to expect."

"You're probably going to feel full. It's like when you put your dick in my puss. I always feel like I'm getting stuffed."

Once it was strapped on her, my heart started to race. I knew what was coming next. "So how do we do this? I just bend over?"

She laughed. "Get on all fours on the bed."

Her wish was my command, and I did just that. The second I was on my knees, she started laughing again.

"Are you laughing at my butthole?"

"I've just never looked at it like this. It's cute."

My cheeks were beet red, but she couldn't see them because I was looking down at the pillow.

I flinched when she put her finger on my butthole, even though her finger was really gentle. She ran it around the hole. It was the first time she had ever touched it. I couldn't believe it. It felt good even without anything going in there. It was the perfect tease.

"How's that feeling?"

"I like it," I told her.

"Are you less scared about me putting it in?"

There's only a little bit of hesitation in me, and then I said, "I think I can handle it, yeah."

Veronica continued teasing me by running her finger over my butthole. The more she did it, the more I felt at ease. And then it stopped. My breath grew rapidly because there was only one other thing that was coming after that.

It was a little cold after she lubed me up. She put a little bit around the hole, and I could hear her putting more on the dildo. The more seconds that were put in between everything, the more my breath grew rapidly.

It happened. It happened faster than I thought it would have. But it was going in my hole. The dildo. It was far bigger when it was going in than how it looked. I hoped that the same rule applied to my dick when I put it in Veronica.

She did it slowly. She was very considerate and gentle. It was like our first time almost except the roles were reversed. As slow as she was going, it also kind of felt like it was going in fast. I could feel my butthole getting stretched. At one point, I was certain that the entire thing was in.

"It's in," she said right after I thought that.

I smiled because it wasn't bad at all. It felt good. It made my dick harder. I wasn't expecting that. I thought that I would have been conflicted somehow. But no, I enjoyed it thoroughly.

"All right, you can start going."

After I said that, she started to thrust slowly. The more she did it, the more I got used to it. I imagine that it must have been like what she felt when I went in and out of her. It was a very intimate thing. Never had I thought being screwed in the butt by my wife would bring me so close to her. But it did.

"Go faster, baby," I said to her.

She followed my instructions, and the penetration made my dick throb. It was a whole different experience. It was like I was feeling it throughout my entire body. It made my toes curl.

"Fuck," I blurted out. "That feels so good."

She somehow maneuvered her way toward my dick while she thrust in and out of me. So she was simultaneously doing that and jerking me off.

Euphoria was the only way I could describe how it felt. Once again, the pleasure was traveling throughout my whole body. It was emanating from my dick, but I knew where to travel. I didn't even feel like I was on the bed anymore. I felt like I was on a cloud. It was a cloud that I never wanted to get off. But I didn't have a choice because the more that she went in and out of me, the closer I got to climaxing.

"You're close to coming, aren't you?"

"Keep going."

She grabbed hold of both my ass cheeks and thrust harder. Three more pumps and I was done for. I curled up almost like a turtle position and started the squirt. She must have hit my G-spot or something because my orgasm was like nothing I had ever felt before.

When it was all over, the sheets were covered in my jizz, and I felt like my muscles were Jell-O.

Looking at Veronica, I saw her smiling at me. It was like she had completed a game of sorts and pulled off this huge feat. "Can't believe we just did that. I fucked you in your butt." She kissed me after saying it.

We cleaned up the bed, and I lay down on my back. I had to return the favor to her. I took off her dildo and started to finger her. There was no way that I was going to get hard again to have sex with her, so I needed to work my magic with my fingers and my tongue.

I watched her nipples stiffen, her body go limp, and her eyes close. Ten years and it was still a mesmerizing sight.

She must have gotten turned on by the pegging because she had gotten close to climaxing super fast. She grabbed hold of one of her titties, and I increased my speed of jerking her off. Faster and faster I went until she froze up and then let out this little scream that told me my mission had been accomplished.

We both lay there next to one another and began to cuddle. She kissed me and buried her face into my chest.

"Ten years in, and you've officially been screwed in the butt by your wife."

I laughed. "In about a half hour, I'm probably going to be ready to go again, and I'm going to do it with you and yours."

He laughed right back, and we continued to cuddle as if we'd only been married for five minutes. I couldn't wait to see what was in store for our twentieth anniversary.

Graduation Day
By Ethan Watkins

Graduation day. I would miss working on Penny's thesis with her. It was about a younger woman and an older man. Being forty-five myself, I couldn't help but put myself in the shoes of the characters she wrote about. That was where I drew the line of my professionalism. It didn't help that the guy in her thesis had also been black.

I watched as Penny took the stage and accepted her diploma. She had such poise and confidence for someone in her early twenties. She was much the character that she wrote about; the woman had such an unbelievable amount of certainty in herself that it almost seemed unrealistic. The only reason that I believed it was because Penny had it herself.

I was glad that I would always have that story on

my computer to reread. Because after graduation, there would be no more Penny. That was a good thing, though. Because I was her professor. I wasn't supposed to have had the little feelings that I did for her, but she was an attractive woman. She had such a sensitive resting face. Her eyes were always so compassionate. I'd be lying if I said that I didn't enjoy my time with her perfecting her thesis. It had turned into this full-length novel and morphed into a rather intimate experience. I usually didn't take thesis projects on for that very reason alone. I didn't care about one-on-one time with students. I enjoyed standing before the class and keeping that distance, not allowing myself to get too close to anyone. Losing a wife a few years back will do that to a person.

In any case, I was happy that I had helped her, able to watch her cross that stage and achieve her goals. It hadn't been easy getting close to her at times, having sexual feelings for her, and watching my guard collapse a little bit. She had a way of getting to know someone whether they wanted her to or not.

As she accepted her diploma, she looked into the crowd and landed in the front row where I had been sitting. When we locked eyes, suddenly it felt like the entire room had emptied and it was just her and me—a dangerous feeling, to say the least. She wore this beautiful smile as if I was the one who single-handedly gave her that diploma.

I wasn't sure what had come over me, but this led me to get from my seat and leave the ceremony. I knew she was done. I knew I would most likely never see Penny Bloom ever again. What I wanted was to forget her, move on and rid myself of the weird feeling that I shouldn't have had. I was squeezed by some people at the exit of the main room of Arthur Ash stadium in Queens and felt the fresh air hit me once I was out. When it came to Penny, she was something I considered a close call. There was no way that I could have allowed myself to get close to a student like that. I could have ruined my career and my life. For some sexual feelings? A crush? It wasn't worth it. Penny had gotten what she wanted. My job was done.

This didn't mean that I didn't think about her after the semester had come to a close. The day of the graduation when I had gone home, she was on my mind constantly just because I knew I would never see her again. I guess there was sadness, but overriding that sadness were thoughts of my ex-wife. Sure, she had divorced me, but six months after that divorce, a car had taken her out. Knowing that my ex-wife had died in such a tragic way, I don't know, there was an immense amount of guilt there. It wasn't easy to just connect with one of my students even if it was on a real level. That was only the first day. It got better as time put itself in between us.

It was only when the first day of the next semester had occurred that everything changed. I had gotten through my day. I taught my classes. As I always did, when the class ended on the first day of the semester, I sat there looking over everyone's first submission and tried to get myself organized. It was like a first-semester ritual. It never changed. Until that day.

There was a knock on my classroom door. It was a light knock. If a feather could knock, that would have been it. When I looked to my left, there she was —Penny Bloom.

It was kind of like when a sitcom character disappears for a bit and comes back looking even better. She was stunning. Her hair had these beautiful curls that looked like she had just been sitting down in a makeup chair for a movie for a few hours. Her smile was there, and yet I had no idea why it was directed toward me.

"Hi, Professor Johnson," she said in the doorway.

I stood up to be polite. I wore a smile shortly after. "Please, call me David now. And come on in."

For the first time since knowing her, I hugged her. It felt taboo, downright illegal. But even so, her citrusy scent threw a party in my nostrils. I didn't want to let go. But of course, I did.

"What brings you here, Penny? How have you been?"

"I've been good. I've been really good. Thanks for your help with my thesis. I would have come to see you sooner, but I knew you weren't on campus."

My adrenaline was pumping just talking to her. There was something different about her aura. It was like she was no longer my student. She still had that friendliness that urged her to get closer to whoever she was talking to, but it was even more so. It was this energy that I could put my finger on. She was just so present with me at that moment. "Well, it's great to see you, Penny. It is. I have thought about you since graduation."

I should have said that it slipped out.

"Have you now?"

What should I say? How do I backtrack from that statement without being creepy? "Yeah, cuz you know we worked on your thesis for a very long time, and I just was always curious as to how that turned out for you. I mean, I know you graduated–"

"Can I tell you something about the thesis? That

long novel that you and I worked on together and perfected."

My brain did this thing where I tried to figure out what she was going to say. I was the type of person that liked to predict things and know what was coming. That was one reason why I was a professor. I enjoyed the structure. I enjoyed having a routine in that I knew what was coming next. But standing with her, I had no idea. "Yeah, of course, you can tell me anything."

"There's a reason that I wrote that book. There's a reason that I use the characters that I used. I write about people that I admire. I write about people that inspire me. And I write about people in whom I'm interested. That's how I base my characters. So if you can't tell, I wrote that main character about you."

I would have pinched myself if it had been socially acceptable to do so. That would have looked weird, though. It was like I was in some sort of dream. The entire semester that I had worked with her, I wanted her. I squashed those feelings down like they were flames in a house. Suddenly, everything that I wanted was presenting itself to me. Or maybe it wasn't. Maybe she would just be overly nice. "You wrote that about me? Now, why would you do that?"

Her eyes went to the floor as she bit her lip. "There's a reason I picked you to work on my thesis with me." Her eyes went back to me. "There's a reason that I had to make the character about you as well. I'm not only interested in you, David, I want you. And I know that would have been wrong a few months ago as your student..."

I couldn't look away from her. I was hooked in the worst of ways. How did I get to the point that I was at?

"But I'm no longer your student. Am I?"

"No. You're not my student anymore. You were a great college student, though. Heck, I couldn't get you off my mind. That's how good you were."

"So if you couldn't get me off your mind, and I can't get you off my mind, what do we do about something like that?"

A pause came to me because whatever action I took next was most certainly going to change my life. "Well in your thesis, there was that scene where both characters gave in to their impulses. You remember that scene, don't you? But I don't know how realistic it is. I don't know if that would happen in real life."

She smiled and stepped toward me. I couldn't believe what was happening. "I think it would happen in real life. I think we can even prove that."

She leaned in and kissed me. I had imagined the moment a million times. And a million times I imagined doing the right thing and pushing her off of me. But I guess in real life things would be different because I didn't push her off at all. I instead pulled her in closer to me and looked out of the corner of my eye to make sure that my door was closed. Did I know what was going to happen next? No. And instead of hating that, I loved it. It was the type of unpredictability that I welcomed.

My hand went to the side of her face, and her hands went to my hips. We pulled each other in closer, and the electricity gave me goosebumps. Dreams did come true apparently. Because my tongue was in her mouth. Hers danced with it. She was a lot feistier than I had imagined. She had far more energy than I could have predicted. It was an incredible thing.

The next thing I knew, our tongues dancing with one another was old news because my hands were on her breasts. She was in a T-shirt and these jean short shorts. But I focused on the T-shirt. As I grabbed her titties, we moved toward the back of my classroom where we would be out of sight. Someone could enter and get me in trouble. But honestly, I couldn't care less. I had everything that I wanted right in front of me. If I had died five minutes later, I would have died a happy man. I had gone from grading papers to making out with the woman who I'd been fantasizing about for almost a year. If there was ever a time to believe in manifesting, it was that one.

Her breast was squishy in my hand. It was shielded by a half-inch bra. That would have to come off soon because the more I touched her, the more I wanted her. She was precious to me. I'm sure she didn't know that, but I would try to express it as much as possible even though what we were doing still felt a little wrong. Sure, she was no longer my student, but she was still my student.

And that student was grabbing my dick through my pants. I was rock solid, so there was no way of hiding it anyway. But my God was her touch aggressive. There was no way to not tell that she wanted me. Being a man who had been through a lot of pain in his life, I couldn't help but wonder what her agenda was. I couldn't just allow myself to believe that she wanted me. Although it sure did seem like that was the case. Usually, a hand on a cock would mean that the person wanted you.

When we were toward the back of the room, I lifted the shirt off of her and laid my eyes on her lacy bra. Her titties were overflowing from the thing, but no nipples were showing. She had such a great body. She was thin but not too skinny.

I ran my fingers up and down her torso before kissing her breasts. I could feel her body soften at that moment. That was how I knew that she was mine. There was no turning back. Reality just wouldn't let us. So I moved forward and unhooked her bra. Her massive titties flopped down about a half inch before I took that bra right off. Before me were these large nipples. Both of them were super hard. I wasted no time putting one in my mouth. Up and down my tongue flicked while I sucked on the center.

"Oh my God," Penny blurted out. Her voice had completely changed for me. She was so sensual, with such a different vibe altogether. It was like I had been transported into a different world altogether. And I loved it. I loved every moment of it.

She started to undo my pants. I didn't stop her. Instead, my heart rate started to quicken. The goose-bumps on my arms all stood up like they were a little army. I couldn't remember the last time I had been so excited. When she took my dick out, she stared at it for a moment. I'd like to think that she was taken aback by how big it was.

Without any warning, she got down on her knees

and started to suck. The goosebumps that I had remained, and they might have even gotten a little stronger. I knew that my dick was getting stronger. It was getting harder with every suck. Her lips were talented. They puffed out with each movement that she did. My veins disappeared now and then as she tried to deepthroat me. It was a stark contrast to the girl I had been working on the thesis with. This was a different girl altogether.

I had been surprised by how close to climaxing she got me. I had been on dates since my ex-wife, and no woman had ever gotten me close to climaxing while giving me head. Penny was a different story. She made me feel like I was younger and less disciplined in my sexual activities.

I had to pull her head off my dick. "I was going to come. But I'd rather come after fucking you."

She smiled with a devious look in her eyes. There again was a whole different woman from what I had been used to. She started to unbutton her jean shorts. I watched every second of it with anticipation. I was moments away from knowing what her pussy looked like. Again, none of it felt real to me.

After the button was open, she unzipped it. There was a split second of seeing her matching underwear to her bra. And then both the underwear and her shorts came down. When she stood up, I got to look at her pussy from the standing position. I could see her little slit right there before me. It was shaved and waiting for me. So I turned her around, bent her over, spread her cheeks, and stuck my dick right in.

It took me a moment to get all the way in as she was super tight. Her wetness helped. The second that I was in, I wanted to pinch myself all over again. She was holding on to one of the desks, and I was looking at her back and her cheeks. Her ass cheeks were gigantic but in the best of ways. I held on to both as I went in and out of her vagina. I moved one of my hands to her hair and gave it a little pull. She seemed to like that as she let out a little moan when I did.

In and out my dick went. Her ass cheeks made waves with every thrust.

The longer I was in there, the closer I got to climaxing. But she climaxed before me. That made me feel good. Her whole body tensed up. She stopped moving altogether, clutching the table as hard as she could. She had to put a hand over her mouth to not scream too loud. This pushed me over the edge, causing me to pull out and finish all over her back.

After we cleaned ourselves up, we quickly got dressed and laughed about how we didn't get caught. In my wildest dreams, I had imagined the moment that we had together. And it happened. People use that expression–never in my wildest dreams—but she had been in them. And it had all came to fruition.

"So I'm no longer a student, but I would like to be someone that goes on a date with you," she said to me.

I chuckled. "I feel like we skipped a few steps, but a date would be nice. No thesis, no college, just you and me."

She smiled at me once more, and I just knew that she and I might have our happy ending. Because after all, that's how her thesis ended.

The Bouncer
By Rick P. Pagano

Of course, it couldn't just be a regular night for Mick. He was a bouncer at a popular nightclub called Lipsticks. A regular night saw its fair share of ruckus and a little bit of drama but nothing too crazy. Every now and then, people would of course bring up Mick's dick. Because Nick had at one time had sex with a woman he had kicked out. She told everyone about how big his dick was. Being six foot eight, he couldn't help it. And the legend was born. That night, the legend was flaring up a little bit more than he would have liked.

Cuz a few yards away outside of the club, there was a group of girls and one guy. They just kept looking in that direction. As a bouncer, he enjoyed ignoring most of the stuff that didn't concern him. If they weren't trying to get in, then it wasn't really hitting business. But these people just kept staring. And it made for a big distraction.

Just because Mick had a giant cock did not mean he had the confidence that went with it. He was a quiet dude. He had a shaved head, a mustache, and plenty of tattoos. But he was a teddy bear on the inside. He didn't like unnecessary attention. As big as he was, he just enjoyed blending into the background.

Without having to listen too closely, he knew that they were talking about his dick. He could tell by one of the girls' eyes, just by the way she was looking at him. Plenty of men imagine having an eight-inch cock. But they don't often think about what comes with that. They don't think about how much of a freak show you become. Sure, it gets you women, but after a while, you start to feel empty. You just start to feel like a giant dick yourself. That's how he felt at times. The novelty of it had worn off. It was no longer fun.

Despite the discomfort that he felt standing there next to those gawkers, he tried his best to ignore it and focus on work. He checked IDs, listened to the music of the club behind them, and just did his own thing. It wasn't as though those people were going to be there all night. That was his technique. When things got bad at work, he reminded himself that it wasn't a forever shift. All bad times came to an end. It was a philosophy he'd kept throughout his life. It helped to be single as well. He still hadn't found love, and that was a bad time for him. But again, all bad times come to an end. He was certain of it.

There was a moment when things died down outside and the group broke off. It was just one girl and that one guy left. They started to look at Mick, and that made him uncomfortable. Just because bad times would come to an end didn't mean that he wasn't allowed to wish that they would come sooner.

Both of them started to walk over to Mick, meaning that it was about to get worse somehow—he could just feel it. He could tell by the look in their eyes what was going to happen. They were probably going to ask to hook up. Or maybe the girl was going to ask to hook up. It wasn't rare for that to happen because of his dick size. At times it made him wonder if he should just get a different job and move. Then again, there are plenty of women who suffered from his plight just because they had big breasts. Those were the reasons why he found it hard to complain about it.

"You're Mick, right? The bouncer with the big dick?" the woman said.

There was something about her voice that captivated me. She also had a look at her. Like when she looked at you, it felt like you were the only person in the world. Her lips were luscious. Whatever gloss she had on had perfectly accentuated them. The guy she was with kind of looked like a punk rock, goth dude. He was far less outgoing than she was. He was still masculine, but she definitely wore the pants in the relationship.

"Yes, that's me. As I tell people a million times over."

"My name is Kim, and this is my boyfriend, Jack. He's a cuckold and wants to see you fuck me. I want him to see what it's like for a real man to fuck me."

Mick couldn't deny the fact that the way she said it intrigued him. She was an alluring individual, to say the least. There was an essence about her that separated her from a lot of other offers. She looked like she really wanted it. Not only that, but her body was killer. He couldn't tell whether or not she had breast implants or her push-up bra was just on fleek. Her curves even looked fake. The hips she had made Mick just want to pull off her pants. So how could he say no? He hadn't had sex in six months since he had broken up with his girlfriend. His girlfriend had fallen into drugs and left a sour taste in his mouth romantically.

"I guess I can make that happen. No, I usually don't make exceptions for such requests."

Kim smiled. "So why are you making an exception for me?"

Mick looked at Jack and then back at her. "I'd rather not disrespect your boyfriend here."

"I won't take any offense. This was all my idea. I want her to fuck you. It's a kink of mine. We've never done this, and I've just been dying to see it happen. When I heard about your dick, there's nothing more than I'd like then to be emasculated in that way, if that makes sense."

Mick gave him an odd look. It wasn't an easy thing for him to understand. It was downright strange. But it was also funny that so many people would open up about their kinks just because he had a big dick. "Well as long as you both are weird about it, I'm on board."

Kim's face lit up. She looked genuinely happy that Mick had obliged. It made Mick feel wanted to a certain extent. Unlike the other hookups he had been offered, there was something genuine about her gaze. There was an aura about her that Nick could not deny. He was actually kind of excited to have sex with her.

He got a call from her two days later. It was to set up their hookup session. There were a few jitters in him when he picked up the phone.

Her voice sounded a little bit deeper and more sultry when they spoke. It turned him on a little bit. His massive dick didn't get extremely hard but a little bit. Of course, he could have denied the thoughts of having sex with her. It was like the elephant in the room. An elephant that he was looking forward to.

"Hello?" Kim said on the other line.

"Hey, what's up?"

"You want to do it tonight? Jack and I are ready. I'm probably going to bring my dildo. Not that I'll need it. But I want you to tease Jack a little bit. I went there to be some build-up before you put your actual dick inside me."

Mick couldn't deny the fact that she was very straightforward with everything that she said. It amazed him how a woman so petite could be so nonchalant about sex. She was small in stature but had a large voice. "You really don't sugarcoat anything, huh?"

"Not at all, sweetheart. What you see is what you

get. I take life and I grab it. I squeeze the hell out of it."

Mick imagined her grabbing his dick. "Are you going to bring that type of energy with my cock? Just because it's big doesn't mean that it needs to be revered. I like a little aggression." Hey, it wasn't easy for someone to be forthright about that type of stuff. But she made it easy.

Kim laughed on the other end. "There's nothing gentle about me. I'll make that big dick of yours look small, I promise. At least in my hands, that's how it'll be."

Goosebumps popped up on Mick's arms.

When the phone call ended, he took a shower and got himself ready. It was funny because even though he was working on his outfit, he knew that the clothes wouldn't be on long. They were going to be torn off by that woman. It was so strange that her boyfriend was just going to sit there and watch. Maybe he would stroke his dick or something. Mick had no idea what he was in for. It definitely wasn't one of those situations that you could predict. There were so many variables and elements that he knew were just going to happen. The less thinking the better.

The drive over to her house wasn't long at all. It

was maybe thirty minutes. Her house was pretty quaint. It had a red roof and a white fence and didn't promote anything that was going on inside that home. You would never think that there were a bunch of swingers in there. You would probably think that there was an old grandma cooking something with jam.

Despite how quiet the house looked, Mick's heart was racing. He couldn't wait to have sex with her. He hoped that he was going to last. Maybe knowing that there was some guy looking at him having sex would elongate the process.

He shut the car off and left it. Walking up to the house, he wiped his clammy hands on his jeans, before ringing the doorbell.

Seconds later, Kim opened the door in a robe. She smiled the second that she saw Mick. He had to remind himself that he was only having sex with her. It wasn't like they were dating. So there were to be no attachments. He couldn't allow that for himself. "Hi, Mick," she said.

"Hi, Kim."

When he looked over her shoulder, he could see Jack in the background. He wasn't standing in a defensive way or anything like that. He just kind of existed. Mick didn't envy the man. There was something so submissive about him. He couldn't understand why a woman like Kim would even want to be with him. But that was none of his business. He was only there to have sex with her.

"Come on in."

Mick stepped inside and felt his shoulders relax because their home was clean and modernly furnished with a black and white farmhouse-type theme. There was nothing creepy about it thus far. He had expected some level of creepiness, but there was nothing.

"How are you guys doing today?"

"I'm good," Jack said.

"Don't mind his lack of dialogue. He's a little nervous to see you fuck me."

There was nothing that could get him used to the way that she spoke. No matter what she said and how many times she said it, he was still caught off guard by her forwardness. "Let's get to it then. Why waste time talking?"

Kim smiled once more. "Bedroom is upstairs." She gestured to the stairs, and they all went up. Mick's heart rate began to jump again. In a way, he couldn't believe what was happening. It was surreal, almost like he was in some sort of movie. Unlike a movie, though, he knew that once it was over, there would be no rewatching it. So he wanted to enjoy the moment. He wanted to revel in it because it wasn't every day that he was smashing some other guy's girlfriend.

When they got to the bedroom, it was spacious. It was a lot of red. The bed looked like it was king-size. The blankets were silky. Jack took a seat in the recliner over in the corner. He opened it up so that he could lean back and get comfortable. "Do you mind if I stroke myself while you do this?"

Mick raised an eyebrow. He wasn't too caught off guard by that because it was kind of what he expected. "No, I don't care."

Jack had been wearing sweatpants. He undid the tie in the front, clutched the waistband, and pulled them down. He did the same with his boxers, his cock springing out. It wasn't super hard yet. But even though it wasn't, Mick could tell how big he was. And she was probably working with around five inches. That let him know that she was definitely not going to be used to the size that he was about to give her.

Jack started to touch himself slowly. That was when Mick looked away. He turned his attention to Kim. She was so beautiful with her plump lips. But it was her body that he was after. He couldn't wait to see what was under that robe.

Mick kicked off his sneakers and took off his T-shirt. Kim ran her hands down his chest and torso, stopping at his belt. He felt himself get hard the second her fingers landed there.

It was then that Mick untied her robe and pulled the thing off her. She was wearing lingerie. It wasn't see-through, so there was still a little bit of mystery. "Do you like what you see?" she asked him.

He nodded yes and gave a squeeze to one of her titties. She had to be a double D. Those things were overflowing. Both she and Mick looked over at Jack. He was stroking a little bit harder. The whole thing was weird, but Mick was still turned on.

"I can't wait to see this big dick of yours."

"So take it out."

Kim followed the order. She unbuckled his massive belt with a little bit of a struggle. Eventually, she got it undone. Then came the button and finally the zipper. She pulled his jeans down first. There was a little bit of an imprint on his boxers. He wasn't fully erect as Jack had become.

"This is a moment of truth, huh? I finally get to see this legend of a dick," Kim joked.

"Come on now; you're going to embarrass me."

She bit her lower lip, bent down, and placed her fingers on the elastic of his boxers. This caused his dick to get really hard. Before he knew it, she was pulling them down. His dick sprang out fast. Her eyes widened at the side of it. All eight inches of him. It was probably more than eight, but he never officially measured it. He just knew that it was way over seven.

"Holy shit," Kim blurted out.

"Damn," Jack added.

It almost made Mick's cheeks go red. "All right, now that you've seen it, let's get that shock value out of the way. It's just a dick."

Kim laughed, bent his dick down, and started to suck. She could barely get it in her mouth. There was no deepthroating that was going to happen there. She could only get one-third of it in between her lips. But it was still good. The way that she sucked made Mick close his eyes.

She had a good rhythm to it. There were moments when she was aggressive, and there were moments when he could feel every inch of her lips. The way she was gentle made him crazy. In between sucks, she would run her finger up and down the shaft just teasing.

"This shit is so big and veiny. It's so much bigger

than Jack's little dick over there. I want to feel it inside of me."

"We can make that happen."

Mick lifted him up and brought her to the bed. He kissed the top of her titty before yanking down the bra. She had very big nipples. Dark ones too. He sucked one while fingering her. At first, he touched her with the underwear on. Then he slipped his fingers beneath it. She was soaked. He had this brief moment where he felt bad that this woman was so turned on by him even though her boyfriend was in the room. In any case, he couldn't wait to stick his rod inside of her. So he pulled her underwear down and shoved it in there. He knew that she liked the little bit of pain that came with pushing his dick into her.

Her eyes nearly bulged out when it was fully in. Her mouth opened wide. Seeing the amount of shock that was on her face, Mick asked, "You okay?" He didn't want to hurt her.

"Yeah. I'm just..."

Mick looked over at Jack, who didn't look too happy that his wife was experiencing such a big dick. But he also didn't seem bitter about it. He just continued to stroke his dick.

"Just in awe of this thing that's in me." She closed her eyes after speaking and said, "Just fuck me."

With the permission given, he started to thrust hard in and out. It wasn't just because his dick was big that it felt tight in there. But it felt really tight in there. At the same time, it was also super wet. The pleasure was beyond anything that he had expected.

He looked at her titties bouncing up and down as he thrust as hard as he could. Every now and then, he would slow down a little bit just to get her more into it. She was a totally different person as he was doing that. It was like she was melting away. Her eyes crossed at that time. She bit her lower lip more times than he could count. There were points where she squeezed her own titty. But the best was when she ran her hands up and down his back. I turned him on to the point where he almost had to pull out because he felt like he was going to finish.

Throughout the entire session, Jack was barely in the room. Mick forgot about him entirely. The cuckold didn't matter at that moment. It was all about them.

"I'm going to come," she blurted out.

Mick smiled. He watched her face scrunch up with pleasure. Her eyes shut so tightly that he thought they would never open.

"Fuuuuck," she said while gnawing at her wrist.

They had gotten what they wanted. The cuckold

had witnessed another man have sex with her. He was another man who had a giant dick way bigger than Jack's. Mick didn't know what the rest of their life was going to look like after that encounter. It would always be a story that they remembered. But it would also be a story that Mick would always remember, because after all, Kim had really turned him on.

Maybe one day he would find his own love. But until then, he would think about her titties every now and then. That was happily ever after enough for him.

Cigar Daddy
By Justin Oliver

Everyone knew me as Kirk, the guy who owned the cigar lounge. But Taylor knew me as Daddy, and I couldn't wait until the damn day ended so that I could have her all to myself.

Damn it, time was going slow. And those curves were killing me. She was my bartender. I had seen her naked plenty of times. But with that crop top, short shorts, and pierced belly button, I was like a caged animal looking at her. I just wanted to reach out and touch her. The fantasy of kissing her neck right below her ear almost made me hard.

"I heard there might be another cigar lounge opening up across town. You know we ain't going to that one." Derek, one of my usual patrons, said it to me as I changed the channel from golf to the football game on the TV in the corner.

"Yeah, screw them. Let them open up a million shops. I know my loyal people keep coming here."

When I said that, my eyes drifted up toward Taylor behind the bar. She was looking at me, biting her lip. I guess the words *loyal people* applied to her. Because she was loyal to me. Sometimes I wondered if it was just because I was paying her way through college. But she didn't have to have sex with me for that! I never wanted her to be my girl just for that. I didn't think that she would have put up with my little kink of always having a cigar when we fucked. She had too much integrity for that. I might have been her daddy, but she was more than just a girl.

"Yeah, man, you run a great ship. There's no other lounge in a town like this one."

Things like that always made me feel good. When it came to my life, I couldn't complain. I had everything that I wanted. And Taylor was part of that equation. She was actually a huge part of the equation. She was the one that kept me sexually satisfied.

"I appreciate that, man. I really do. I'll try to run the best cigar lounge that I can."

The guy went off to his friends, and I walked over to Taylor. It was only a certain amount of time that I could tolerate being away from her.

"I knew you were going to come over here at some point. You can't go ten minutes without being around me," Taylor said with a devious smile. She knew she had me by the balls even though I was her daddy. We had such a funny dynamic.

"Of course. I just fuckin' love smelling you. Today has dragged on, girl. I just wanted it to be over with." I feel bad saying that, given the fact that my lounge was my life. I should have always been grateful for it. In what other job could you smoke cigars all day? It's just that my bartender made it hard for me to want to work.

"Why do you want the shift then so bad?" She said it in a playful voice because she knew damn well why I wanted it to end.

"Cuz I want to go to bed," I joked. She couldn't tell. "I'm kidding. You know I want to fuck you." I pulled the cigar out of my mouth and aimed the cloud of smoke over my shoulder. She leaned in. I could never really tell if she just tolerated the smoke or it turned her on. I suspected the latter, which wound me up even more.

She put on her serious face. God, she was fucking beautiful. "Well, you're just going to have to wait. You know I'm wearing the lacy panties that you got me."

There went my dick going hard all over again. I had to press it up against the counter to not let anyone see. The way that she controlled me was incredible. I was a full-grown man, yet she drove me like I was a car.

"What's the matter? You're getting hard."

Holy crap. "Shhh, we have to be professional. But yeah. I'm trying to make it go away."

"If I make it worse, are you going to come in your pants?"

"Cut it out, girl; I'm going to walk away."

"What, you don't like thinking about my hard nipples right now? You know my little pink nipples that you love putting in your mouth." The voice she was using was a cross between a whisper and a sultry tone.

"All right, I'm going to walk away." I tried to, but she held on to my hand.

"Don't go. I'll stop. I hate when you're away from me, Daddy."

It might have been the first time in my adult life

that I ever came in my pants with the way she was talking to me. "Hey, don't call me that right now. You're really going to make me come."

She giggled and let go of my hands, and someone walked up to the counter. "Let me get a whiskey on the rocks."

She looked at me when she said, "Coming right up." I smiled through the cigar in my jaw and went to attend to a customer in the walk-in humidor.

There were two hours left until the shift was over; then I could lock up, and I could spread her legs. I thought about that pussy for the whole two hours. It might have sounded like I had a problem, but the truth of the matter was, her pussy was just that good. No matter how many times I hit it, it was like the first time.

I watched her do her job from my office. I had the perfect view via my one-sided mirror. I could see the staff and they couldn't see me. She knew that I looked at her though. She knew that I studied her. Because Taylor was a whole different type of woman. She had an aura that you just couldn't forget. No matter how much time you spent away from her, she lingered. She had power about her. It was a power that most women dreamed of—and not just to get with men, just overall confidence that you couldn't duplicate or engineer.

Lucky for me, though, time ticked on, and eventually, it was time to close up.

"Have a good night, Louie. Thanks for coming by," I said as Louie walked through the door. He was another one of my longtime patrons. I locked the doors and closed the curtains of the shop. They were more like blinds, long blinds that ran from the ceiling to the floor. Knowing that it was just me and Taylor there, my heart started to race.

"Well, would you look at that, you survived the shift without coming in your pants," she said to me as I turned around.

"You are a real bad girl, aren't you?"

She giggled as she cleaned up her bartender spot. "You know you like me as a bad girl, though. You wouldn't have it any other way, Big Daddy."

I laughed. She really always knew how to tickle my funny bone. But she knew how to tickle my dick a lot better.

I walked over to the counter and walked behind it. The next thing I did was grab her by her hip and pull her in close to me. I finally got the kiss that I had been waiting for all day. Her body softened when I pulled her in close to me. She became such a mush with my touch.

"You know I'm happy that the day's over too," she said in a low tone.

"Yeah? Cuz sometimes I feel like I want it more than you."

She looked at me and raised an eyebrow. She might have even been a little offended. "How can you say such a thing? You're my daddy, and you know that."

"I'm also your daddy who pays for your college."

"No, because I earn that by working here. If I didn't really enjoy you, you know I would work in any other cigar lounge that had me. I can even work at Hooters; they would take me without batting an eye."

I couldn't tell if she was trying to make me jealous or if she was just being honest. Either way, I liked her fire. "That's a really valid point. You have the brains and beauty to work wherever you want to, and you choose to work with me. I don't know if that just doesn't make sense."

She shook her head while wiping down a glass. The way that she cleaned it reminded me of the way that she stroked my dick. Her hands were just so sure of themselves. "You're such a successful man. You have everything that you've ever wanted in your life, and you doubt that you deserve any of it. But you treat me better than anyone has ever treated me. In any relationship that I've ever been in, I was always treated like a piece of meat. Sure, you treat me like that as well. But you treat me like that with love in your eyes, a passion where I know that you're taking care of me while also fucking me."

The way she spoke sent me into a place similar to paradise. "I'm really glad you see all that, but I think that this time stop talking and let the actions take over."

She smiled, put her glass down, and gave me a long kiss. The second that her tongue entered my mouth, I started getting harder. There was no control over it. Her hands ventured to the back of my salt-and-pepper, close-cropped hair. She didn't know this, but I kept it that way because I knew that she liked the feeling of a fresh cut. She also liked my mustache, so I kept that too.

While she had me lean up against the counter, I squeezed her titty, and she let out a moan. Her lips went a little bit faster when I did that. She enjoyed my animalistic side. When she could turn me into that horn dog, driven by lust and desire, it turned her on to no end. And I knew this because when my hand went down there, where her little short-shorts sat, she was soaked through them.

"Damn, you're wet," I said to her.

"Why do you seem so surprised? I'm always wet when I'm with my daddy."

I didn't say anything in return. Instead, I put my fingers beneath her underwear and started to stroke her little clitoris. I knew all the motions that she enjoyed. The second that I started doing that, she'd stop moving altogether just to enjoy it. She was completely at the whims of my fingertips. What could be better than that? I squeezed her titty while I did that to her. She moved her body closer to me. I switched from grabbing her titty to grabbing her ass. The cheeks separated when I did that. My patience went out the window.

"One second, Daddy. Did you forget your favorite part?" She walked over to the small, private humidor I keep under the bar, and pulled out my cigar. I called it *my* cigar, because I've been working with a famous cigar roller to create my own blend. I am incredibly proud of this stick, and I can't wait to get enough produced to share them with my customers.

Before I knew it, she had clipped the end of the unbanded cigar, a 60-ring maduro, and put it between her teeth. She smiled at me, and like a pro, grabbed the torch lighter from the bar and fired it up. She took a few puffs to make sure it was lit. Fuck, watching that turned me on. She handed me the cigar. "Now where were we?

Bending down, her shorts seductively came off along with her underwear. I watched her, my cigar in my jaw. Rock fucking hard. "What are you waiting for, Daddy?"

I held my cigar in my hand and got closer to that perfect cunt. Licking her while she stood there was everything to me. Never would I get fatigued of her flavor. That warm saltiness was what I lived for. There was so much of it because of how wet she was. She was quenching my thirst, a party for my tongue.

Taylor ran her fingers through my hair as I ate her out. She spread her legs farther and farther for me, just so I could get a better angle. This led me to stick my fingers in her. I had no trouble getting them in. She was perfectly lubricated naturally. With each movement that I made with my fingertips, she became limper, needing to hold on to the counter. It was crazy to me how such a perfect woman could become so submissive in my presence. I loved this so much.

I took a puff on my cigar and exhaled right on her

cunt as I kept working. Her moan told me that she enjoyed this as much as I did.

But then I guess she had enough because she picked me up and undid my pants. "Enjoy your cigar, Daddy. I'll help you relax." She lowered herself to my raging hard dick.

Her lips moved up and down my cock, my hard cock. I watched it because I loved to watch it. It was like she had superpowers when she sucked my dick. I held my cigar in my jaw and put my hands behind my head. Fucking perfect moment.

She had both her hands on my ass cheeks. She was really going in on me. With every suck that she gave me, I felt more wanted. I felt desired. Every now and then, she would pull me closer so she could get more of my dick in her mouth. Her eyes were closed, and her entire face looked different every time she had her lips wrapped around me. I gently caressed her face and ran my fingers through her hair.

I let her suck me off a little bit more. Right before I was about to come, I pulled her head off me. She smiled because she knew exactly why I had done that.

"Can't take the heat?" she asked.

I smiled with reddened cheeks. "No, I can't. Not when you bring the heat."

I picked her up, knocked everything off the counter, and laid her down there. I gave her a few more licks because I just had to. Then I stuck my dick in her. She let out this little moan as if she had stubbed her toe. She liked it, though.

With the cigar tight in my teeth, I held the back of her head as I fucked her. Her titties moved up and down even with the shirt and bra on. I lifted both of them up to just see one of her tits. There was her little pink nipple in front of me. The little dots were hard as rocks. The center was equally hard. I put the cigar in my left hand and exhaled a cloud of smoke onto her tit as I took it into my mouth.

"Oh yes, Cigar Daddy. Just like that."

Hearing her talk like that made me throb. I could hear that voice a million times and it would never get old.

Pulling her in closer to me, there was no holding back my urge to go faster while screwing her. Her legs wrapped around my torso. Her hands went to my hips. It was a bond that could not be duplicated in any way. There was no girl out in the world that could match what Taylor brought to the table.

Sucking on her titty, thrusting in and out,

listening to her moan, watching her facial expressions as my dick did its thing, time slowed down. But the pressure on my cock grew more. There was no stopping my climax. No matter what I was going to do or think about, I was too turned on.

I pulled my dick out of that magnificent cunt, put the cigar back in my mouth, and sat back on the bar on my knees.

She knew to reach down, grab my wet dick, and start stroking. She looked me dead in the eyes, and I admired her body though the cloud of smoke around us. She didn't have to do much to get my cock to convulse. Out came all my jizz all over her stomach. Some of it shot up onto her face. It was a strong orgasm to where I couldn't even move for a couple of seconds. I'd nearly bitten through my cigar too—the classic sign of a perfect orgasm.

When it was all said and done, I looked down at my jizz on her belly and her cheek. Her pussy was still glistening. The only difference was that she was smiling and almost laughing. "Well, someone didn't last long."

I shook my head. "I couldn't help it, Taylor. That shit was great."

She finally let out that laugh while sitting up. I pushed her back down.

"I want you to come."

"Take your best shot." She opened her legs for me. My dick was going soft, but that didn't stop me from fingering her. It was still so soaked. My fingers went in and out with ease. I knew what spot to hit. I knew where her G-spot was. It was the roof of her pussy. All I needed was a little bit of pressure.

"Oh my God," she said. "Yes, just like that. Keep going."

I had to maintain the rhythm. Even though I wanted to because it was a natural instinct, I had to keep pace. Some of my cigar ash fell onto her stomach. My instinct was to apologize, but fuck, I think she liked it. The very next moment, her body tensed up, and there was more fluid coming out of her. I guess I had made her squirt.

"Daddy, yes! Fuck, yeah, Cigar Daddy!"

Mission accomplished. I took a big, final puff of my cigar, now smoked down to a nub, and smiled, feeling like a king.

After we cleaned each other up and got dressed, we sat at one of the tables together just drinking whiskey. "This is real life. Even if I don't amount to any of my dreams that I have in college, this is still everything I've ever wanted, Kirk."

"Same for me. If this all went away tomorrow, as

long as I have your ass in my hands, I'm a happy man."

We both laughed at that as we downed our whiskey. She was my little, and I was her daddy. I liked that dynamic. And she liked it too. Maybe there would actually be round two.

The Professional
By Jayson Morris

It was Theresa's six-month divorce anniversary. Never did she think she would be celebrating such a milestone. Like many others, she always dreamed about celebrating her tenth marriage anniversary, and ironically enough, she had only made it to nine years. Those were little things that could drive any cynical person mad. But she wasn't cynical and liked to stay positive; she always tried to look at life in a glass-half-full type of way. That was harder to do given the fact that she was 40 years old. Getting back into the dating scene would be difficult. And then you top it off with being an African American woman in an overly white corporate workplace; sometimes, she didn't know where she fits in in her life. She used to have her marriage and then she had work. Some would call her a workaholic. So if that was the only life that she had left, it was going to be an uphill battle.

And that uphill battle wasn't waiting to get started. This was because she was at a work event. A work event in Atlantic City. And the worst part about it all was that she wasn't allowed to gamble. She worked for a digital marketing firm, and they had paid for the entire trip. But going to gamble would technically be considered gambling on company time. So instead of having fun, it was all just networking, spreadsheets, and coffee. She didn't know what hurt most, the fact that she used to go to Atlantic City with her husband David all the time and was now watching happy couples sip their drinks and win money or the fact that she was there working and wishing that she wasn't.

As she walked the Caesars casino floor to get to a newly added conference area, she hadn't been paying attention and bumped right into a tower of a man. Initially, judging by his suit, she thought maybe he was with the company. Maybe he was a higher-up or something. But then she noticed the luggage that he was pulling behind himself. His suit was too fancy even for the company she worked for. And he smelled delicious. It was a cross between apple cinnamon and some sort of spice.

"Oh man, I'm so sorry. I should have been watching where I'm going. I haven't been to this hotel in a long time," the man said. His voice was deep and sultry. Even with the sounds of colorful machines blaring in the background, all she heard was his tone. She was instantly intrigued, frozen in time.

"It's okay. I wasn't looking either."

The man looked over to the bar. It was another added thing to the Caesars casino that she hadn't been to. It was a place she never went with David. "You don't look like you're in a rush. You want to grab drinks?"

The audacity to just outright ask a stranger for drinks. She thought that only happened in the movies. She was almost offended by how confident he was compared to how down in the dumps she sometimes felt. But of course, her answer was, "I mean, I'm not supposed to be drinking; I'm at a work thing. But I would like to grab a drink."

The man laughed. Something about that made her feel accomplished. He was an older white male who had specks of gray in his hair. It wasn't much but enough to make him look sophisticated and suave. He had a five o'clock shadow, but it didn't look like he was unkempt. It looked more like it was supposed to be there. "I admire your ability to talk through things like this, but I think you should live in a moment. One drink won't kill you."

"One time won't kill us. I shouldn't have done it. I didn't mean to cheat on you," she remembered her ex-husband saying.

"I don't know. I don't typically do this."

The man gave her his eyes. They seem to be understanding. "You know what, I think it was in my approach. I didn't even give you my name. I'm Edmund. Edmund Chestnut."

Theresa shook her head. "There's no way that's your real name."

Edmund laughed. "It's my real first name. It's not my last name. We can talk about that over drinks. I would love to have your name as well."

"Okay, my name is Theresa. Theresa Walnut."

Edmund laughed all over again as they began to walk to the bar. "Let me guess, that's not your real last name either."

"Two can play at that game. Why should I give you my last name if you don't give me yours? Not that they matter."

She thought about how she was supposed to be going to a presentation for work. She did have some time, but she liked to be there early. Edmund was throwing her off completely.

When they sat down at the bar, his presence was god-like. He had such a command of his area. He sat there with confidence by not even doing a single thing. All he did was exist, and there was an air about him that she had never encountered from anyone else before. Her intrigue started to spike. She couldn't care less about his real last name. But she did care about why he felt the need to hide it. Perhaps it was just because they were strangers. But something told her there was more to the story.

"You don't seem like someone that gets out a lot. No offense," Edmund said.

"I don't get out a lot. I'm divorced. Ever since my marriage ended, I kind of became a homebody. I just hang out with my friends, and that's it. Other than that, I'm a workaholic. This is a work trip. I'm not even here to gamble or anything. They have this backward roll where if they're paying for your entire trip, you can't gamble or drink or anything like that. They're the top marketing firm in the world, and they're strict with their employees, especially on business trips. I think in the past there have been a few employees who did some stupid shit and messed it up for everyone.

"Well, I'm here on business too, in a way. I'm an escort."

She hadn't even put her drink in yet, and Theresa swallowed. "An escort?"

"Hey guys, when can I get you?" the bartender intervened.

"I'll have a scotch on the rocks," Edmund said.

"I'll have a strawberry daiquiri."

"Okay, I'll have that right to you." The bartender took her leave, and Theresa didn't quite know how to act. The words wouldn't even come to her.

"Did I catch you off guard?" he asked.

"A little bit. I've only heard of female escorts. So you have sex for money?"

"No. That's a prostitute. And escort is someone who gets paid to hang out. Dinner, companionship, you name it. It's a very specific need."

"And that's what you're here in Atlantic City for?"

"Yes, ma'am. I have a female client who I'm supposed to meet tomorrow."

"I see." She was once again at a loss for words as the bartender brought their drinks. She downed hers in one shot. "I'm not really into that type of stuff, so maybe this was a bad idea."

Edmund chuckled. "Before you leave, do you like your job?"

"It pays very well."

"You didn't answer the question, though."

Theresa stared at the counter for a moment. "I have my bad days at work, and one of them is today before I started talking to you. As weird as I find it that you're an escort, I'm enjoying my time."

"So then go with the flow for once. I can tell that it's hard for you to let loose. I'm not being an escort with you. I think you're gorgeous, and I stopped my day to chat with you, nothing more and nothing less."

Theresa couldn't argue his philosophy. He was right. It was hard for her to let loose at times. If she wasn't thinking about work, she was thinking about how she was a divorced woman. All she wanted to do was let loose and forget about all that. "How do I know that I can trust you? For someone as confident as you who stops me in the middle of the casino, you look like a professional player."

Edmund laughed, nearly spitting up his scotch. "I am a professional player, and I guess I know how to be charismatic, but again, I'm not turning any of that on with you. See, that's the problem with my line of work. People hear what I do and then they become insecure and think that I'm not being real with them or I want to use them for something."

There was a buzzword in that sentence that she hung on to. "I'm the furthest thing from being insecure. I just don't want my time wasted, that's all."

"How about we head up to my hotel room and I show you that I'm a gentleman? And I'm not just out to use you."

"Why bring me up to your hotel room if you're not going to use me?" she teased. "I have a lot of trust issues; it's not just because you're an escort."

"All the more reason to come up to my hotel room so I can prove to you that not all men are scum. And not all escorts are fake."

She laughed and ordered another daiquiri. After downing the cup once more, she followed Edmund up to his hotel room. When she was with him, it was like her job didn't matter. She'd been so fearful of everything, including gambling on the job, and yet there she was going up the elevator with some man she had just met. She couldn't tell whether it was her doing or his charisma.

When they were in his room, he put his luggage by the table and sat down on the chair. There was nowhere else for her to send other than the edge of the bed. She had goosebumps and didn't know why. It wasn't like they were going to have sex.

"See, nothing to worry about," Edmund joked.

"Well, when you say something like that, it makes me worry."

Edmund nodded. "You're right. This isn't natural. I guess as an escort. Sometimes I get lonely. And bumping into you was different. I'm around so many people all the time. You get to know someone's character right off the bat after a while. And I could tell with you, you were a genuine person. I guess even though people can feel expendable to me, I still have that hopeless romantic part of me there somewhere."

"So you do see me in that sexual way then. Did you just bring me up here to have sex with you?"

"Not. You can go, honestly. I just wanted to get to know you, that's all. Feel free to leave if you'd like."

Theresa analyzed his statement. And he was being genuine. She could get up and go right to the door without him batting an eye. "I sense something genuine about you as well."

She rose from the edge of the bed and walked over to him. "You say you get lonely on these trips, but do you have a woman back home? I don't know if that's a stupid question given your line of work." She regretted not asking it before going up to his room. That last thing she wanted was to become someone's mistress, let alone an escort's mistress.

"I don't have anyone back home. That's one reason why I still do this job. It keeps me occupied and keeps me on my toes."

Theresa wasn't someone who traveled to the edge. She rarely ever took risks. But at that moment, she knew that she would never get an opportunity to do something like what she was about to do at that moment.

She walked over to Edmund and kissed him without a moment's hesitation. There was a split second of wondering whether or not he was going to kiss her back or would he push her off and disgusted. Those two seconds were everything because the last person she'd ever kissed was her ex-husband. And Edmund's lips felt euphoric.

He didn't push off. Instead, he pulled her in by her ass cheeks. His firm grip instantly made her wet. Her body grew less stiff and more comfortable with every second that their lips played with one another. Moments later, their tongues were sharing a dance.

It was easy to get on his lap with the chair that he was in. And that's what she did. Running her fingers through his hair, he gave her ass a nice squeeze. She already felt like she was his in a way like he would dominate her. She needed more. So she grabbed him by the collar and left his lap to pull him over to the bed. Her back hit the mattress he got on top of her and started to kiss her neck. She was butter and his presence.

His meaty fingers began to unbutton her blouse. One by one, the buttons came loose and eventually, her lacy bra entered the room. He wasted no time in yanking it down and putting a nipple in his mouth. Her nipples were large and dark. He made them hard. But they were no match for his lips.

Lifting her, he unhooked the back of the bra and took off her dress shirt. When the bra came off, both her tits fell to the sides. But he caught them and gave them an equally hard squeeze. Theresa let out a moan when he did that. She had no control over the sounds that she made.

Returning the favor, she unbuttoned his shirt. The more that she did, the more chiseled muscles appeared to her. For a man who was in his mid-40s, his abs looked like he was in his twenties. Another thing she had no control over was running her hands over those. They were firm, hard like rocks. Warm rocks that had a leathery feel to them. She leaned up and gave them a little kiss. That led to her next move: unbuckling his pants.

She just knew that he had a big cock. She could tell without even looking at it. The belt came on the buckle. The button came undone. The zipper came down. Wasting no time, she pulled his pants down along with his boxers. They made eye contact before her eyes drifted down to his long, thick, veiny, reddish dick. He was throbbing. He was even bigger than she thought. When she wrapped her fingers around it, they barely could fit.

"Fuck," he blurted out. Theresa couldn't help a smile. She was the one in control at that moment. Stroking gently and then harder, she watched his face morph into a mask of pleasure. That big dick of his was hers. It was a monster, and yet she was taming it, moving it every which way, jerking it up and down. It lost a bit of size in her hands because of how aggressive she was.

Harder, harder, it just kept getting harder. Right before it seemed to reach its max, he moved her hand away.

"You were going to come?"

He nodded in shame. But then smiled because he knew what was coming next. He yanked down Theresa's skirt with her underwear. The breeze of the room tickled her clitoris. The next thing she knew, his tongue was in between her legs.

Her eyes closed shut as she moved her hands into Edmund's hair. She gave it a little pull as his tongue flicked at her clit. It had no remorse and did as it pleased. But everything that hit his tongue did; she felt it throughout her whole body. Right before she was about to climax herself, he pulled off and inserted his cock into it.

At first, the thing had a hard time going in, and it was almost painful. But once his cock was inside her, she left her body completely.

"Oh my God, fuck me," she said.

When he started to thrust, it was a whole different experience for Teresa. Up and down her body went as her titties flung all over the place. She was shifting on that bed like she had no weight. And it was all because of his dick. He grunted now and then. Its muscles flexed since he went in and out of her. She could have sworn that she felt her dick in her stomach. He was going so hard. But she liked every moment of it because he would also switch it up and go slow. Those were the times when she felt close to climaxing.

It was around the third time that he started to go

hard that her body tensed up, her toes curled in, and she climaxed, raking her nails along his back.

He continued to thrust for a few more pumps. When he pulled out, his face shifted into one where every muscle was being used. She looked down, and he was holding his dick. It was throbbing in his hands while squirting all over her stomach. Some of it reached her titty. Mission accomplished.

They snuggled in the bed after that. His arm was draped over her chest, and her leg was draped over his leg.

"Sorry if we moved fast," Edmund said. "I swear that what just happened wasn't my intent when I brought you up here."

"Stop apologizing. I came here to work, and this happened. I have no regrets."

"Neither do I. You know, if it ever happens again between us, or if we continue to see each other after leaving this room, maybe I won't need to be an escort."

"And maybe I won't need to be a workaholic."

Only time would tell whether or not they would pursue each other. But based on how they were in that bed, it sure looked like they would.

Afterword

Well, dear friend, I hope you enjoyed this collection of sexy stories written by men for women. I think it's something else!

As always, feel free the send me any feedback you have. I love to hear about your experience with the material.

And while we're on the subject, if you could take 30 seconds to leave a review, it would be a giant help. The more reviews we have, the more people can find the book. Thank you so much in advance for doing that, my friend; it really makes a big difference.

And don't forget to check out my other collections on Amazon and Audible. Just search for "Rayna Russell."

And feel free to submit stories for consideration

in the next collection. Three thousand words is just about perfect.

I'll see you soon.

With outrageous appreciation,
    Rayna

RaynaRussellErotica@gmail.com

www.ingramcontent.com/pod-product-compliance
Lightning Source LLC
Chambersburg PA
CBHW071939190726
48293CB00004B/1283